BRED BY THE SLUMS 3

Lock Down Publications and Ca$h
Presents
Bred by the Slums 3
A Novel by *Ghost*

Lock Down Publications

P.O. Box 870494
Mesquite, Tx 75187

Visit our website @
www.lockdownpublications.com

Copyright 2018 by Bred by the Slums 3

First Edition May 2018
Printed in the United States of America

Lock Down Publications
Like our page on Facebook: Lock Down Publications @
www.facebook.com/lockdownpublications.ldp
Cover design and layout by: **Dynasty Cover Me**
Book interior design by: **Shawn Walker**
Edited by: **Sunny Giovanni**

Stay Connected with Us!

Text **LOCKDOWN** to 22828 to stay up-to-date with new releases, sneak peaks, contests and more…

Thank you.

Submission Guideline.

Submit the first three chapters of your completed manuscript to ldpsubmissions@gmail.com, subject line: Your book's title. The manuscript must be in a .doc file and sent as an attachment. Document should be in Times New Roman, double spaced and in size 12 font. Also, provide your synopsis and full contact information. If sending multiple submissions, they must each be in a separate email.

Have a story but no way to send it electronically? You can still submit to LDP/Ca$h Presents. Send in the first three chapters, written or typed, of your completed manuscript to:

LDP: Submissions Dept
Po Box 870494
Mesquite, Tx 75187

DO NOT send original manuscript. Must be a duplicate.

Provide your synopsis and a cover letter containing your full contact information.

Thanks for considering LDP and Ca$h Presents.

DEDICATION

This book is dedicated to my precious, beautiful Babygirl. The love of my life, 3/10. Everything I do is for YOU, first and foremost.

ACKNOWLEDGEMENTS

I would like to thank the Boss Man and C.E.O of LDP, Cash. Thank you for this opportunity. Your wisdom, motivation and encouragement are appreciated. Thanks, bruh.

To the Queen and C.O.O of LDP, thank you for all that you do, sis. Your hard work, dedication and loyalty to this company never goes unnoticed.

Ghost

Chapter 1

Nikki winced in pain, then jerked real hard against me. I wrapped her more protectively in my left arm, as I raised the Tech with my right, slowly aiming it upward at the Mexican killa who was dead set on killing Nut. As he looked down at Nut, getting ready to send him to the other side, I leveled the weapon, squeezing the trigger, feeling the Tech spit rapidly. *Boom-boom-boom-boom!*

The bullets flew into the side of his face and knocked him off his feet. He fell along side of Nut with his eyes wide open and blood gushing from the holes that my Tech had given him.

I lowered my weapon and looked down to Nikki, who had her eyes closed tight. I could tell she was in pain. I didn't know where she was hit exactly, but I was sure that she was. I tried to sit up and felt a stinging in my left shoulder. I looked down and saw blood pouring out of me as if my shoulder was a faucet. The adrenalin coursing through me wouldn't allow for me to feel any pain and I was thankful for that.

Another truck pulled up outside of the window, and more Mexicans got out of it with assault rifles in their hands. They stopped and kneeled on the concrete, blasting in our direction, trying to pick up where their homies had left off. I covered Nikki with my body as the shots rang out rapidly.

Thot-thot-thot-thot! Boom! Boom! Boom! Boom! Thot-thot-thot-thot-thot! Pee-yon! Pee-yon! Pee-yon! Their bullets slammed into the walls, knocking big chunks of plaster out of it. Smoke filled the air and made it hard for me to breathe. I worried that if they came through the window that had been shot out that they would kill us. I had to protect Nikki. I had to make sure that Nut didn't get hit up more than he already had, but there was nothing that I could do to save either of us. We were under the gun and well outnumbered.

Thot-thot-thot-thot-thot! Boom! Boom! Boom! Errrruh! Vrooooom! Errrruh!

"Shit, Vato! It's a hit!" I heard somebody holler. Then, I heard so many gunshots that it made me fearful to open my eyes.

Boom-boom-boom-boom-boom-boom-boom-boom! Bow! Bow! Bow! Bow! Bow!

"Snake ass niggaa!"

Boom-boom-boom-boom!

I could hear men crying out in pain, and then somebody was patting me on the back. I looked up and into the face of Taurus.

His face was scrunched, and even though he appeared to be on business, he was still dressed in an expensive Gucci suit. "Get up, man, and let's get the fuck out of here. That bitch ass nigga Vito tried to set me up and have me executed. Come on!" He yanked me to my feet, and the next thing I knew, he and about fifteen of his goons were helping me, Nikki and Nut into a Navigator truck.

"Look, Taurus, every one of us got hit by bullets, man, so you gotta take us to the hospital right now. Please!" I hollered, feeling Nikki shake in my arms. I was praying that she was okay and that the bullets didn't hit any of her vital organs. Once again, I didn't even know where she was hit at this time if at all.

Taurus turned around from the passenger seat as we drove away from the scene in a hurry. Sirens blared somewhere off in the distance, and not only was I worried about bleeding to death, now I was worried about the police pulling us over and everything catching up with me at once. I had so many bodies under my belt at this time that I knew for a fact they would put me to sleep.

"I'ma take y'all to Mount Sanai. I know a few of the doctors up in there. I'll make sure that they take care of y'all without reporting this shit to the local authorities. Don't worry. I got everything under control," he said, picking up his phone and dialing a number.

Before the shootout, Simone had sent word to me that I needed to get home because the Pastor was there and supposedly trying to kill my mother. As much as my shoulder was killing me, I had to get over there. I didn't have time to think about myself in that moment. I needed to make sure that the women in my family were safe and sound.

My mother had recently ripped the Pastor off, taking more than $100,000 from the church so that I could step out into the Dope Game of Cloverland. I was guessing that he had somehow found out and was now making her pay for it.

"Say, Taurus, I need you to get them to the hospital, but I need you to drop me off at the corner of my crib. I got some business to take care of. It's important," I said, sliding my arm from around Nikki.

She continued to keep her eyes closed, with her face scrunched. "Shemar, what the fuck are you saying? You gotta go get that bullet out of you right now." She sounded as if she were out of breath and drained.

"Yeah, Shemar, you can always handle that business later. I'm finna invest too much shit into you to have you pass the fuck out and die. First, get that bullet removed, then get stitched up, and you can go wherever you need too, long as you report back to me and we can get a move on. That nigga Vito gotta pay. Nobody crosses me and lives to tell about it. Believe that." He curled his upper lip and lowered his eyes.

I shook my head. "N'all. Fuck that. Look, my crib coming up in three blocks. Just drop me off on the corner and give me one of them hand pistols. I'll meet y'all in an hour. I gotta make sure my people straight, first and foremost. I could give a damn about me."

Nikki shook her head and placed her hand over the right side of her ribs. "Please, just stay, Shemar. I won't be able to calm down unless I know you're beside me. I need you right now. I'm begging you." She opened her eyes and laid her head on my shoulder.

I leaned down and kissed her forehead. "I love you, Nikki, but I gotta do this. Look, Taurus, drop me off, and watch over my heart right here. I'll meet back up with y'all in a minute. This lil' bullet ain't finna stop me. I been through worst. Trust me."

There was a strong throbbing pain in my shoulder, but I refused to let it hobble me in any way. I started to think about Purity— my little sister, and my heart and soul. I couldn't let the Pastor do nothing to her if I could prevent it. It was my job to protect her with all that I was. Then, there was Simone— my foster sister who was pregnant with my child. Just as much as I was supposed to protect Purity, I was supposed to protect her as well. That was my duty as a man.

While the truck rolled on, Taurus took off his seatbelt, and came to the back with us after sliding a yellow first-aid kit from the bottom of his passenger's seat. He came over to me and grabbed my arm, pulling my shirt over my head, then addressed my wound. "Here. Pop these pills while I handle this business. I can't do much, but I at least want to stop it from bleeding so bad."

I opened my mouth, and he dropped two pills onto my tongue. I started to chew them right away with my face balled up. They tasted horrible, but I just wanted the pain to stop. "Ahhhh! Shit!" I hollered as he started to do his thing. I closed my eyes and took deep breaths.

"I'm just sterilizing it, then I'ma stitch it up real fast. You still got a bullet in here, but at least it won't be bleeding so bad. You gon' have to handle yo' business and get at me in less than an hour."

Taurus didn't let me out of that truck until he'd sewn my arm up as best he could, then he handed me a .9-millimeter pistol. I kissed Nikki on the forehead, jumped out of the truck and ran full speed down the block until I got to my house. I went along the gangway, stopped outside of my bedroom window, climbed onto the Electric Company meter box right there, opened my window and fell into my room on my back, making sure that the floor didn't meet my injured shoulder. I heard the commotion right away. I was surprised that it was still taking place.

"Daddy, please let her go. She's had enough. Please." Simone whimpered. She sounded like she was crying, and that made me feel some type of way.

"Please, Vincent, if you hit her again, you're going to wind up killing her," Purity said, sounding as if she were closer to my bedroom than Simone was.

"Both of you, get the fuck back! I'm not going to tell you again! Now, this is my wife. She stole from me, and by the laws of the Bible I have a right to discipline her in any way that I want, until I think she's had enough. Do you get that?" he hollered as I climbed to my feet.

I slowly opened the door to my room and peeked out into the dining room. I could see the Pastor straddled over my mother, holding her by the throat. Her face looked to be battered and bloodied. He was dressed in a white beater, leaving his muscles exposed. Simone stood less than ten feet away from them, while Purity was right outside my doorway with a concerned look on her face.

My shoulder throbbed painfully, but at the same time, I could tell that whatever pills Taurus had given me were starting to take effect.

I cocked back the .9 millimeter and opened the door slowly, creeping out. The first person to see me was Purity. Her eyes got bucked, and I held one finger to my lips, telling her to be quiet. She nodded in agreement, then I trained my eyes back on the scene of the Pastor straddling my mother.

He raised his hand and brought it down against her face again. "Bitch, tell me where my money is, now!"

Simone dropped to her knees with tears running down her cheeks. "You're killing my mother, dad. I can't believe this. You're actually going to do it!" she cried, then put her face against her stomach, rocking back in forth.

"Simone, I already told you to take your ass back into your room. Now I'm not going to tell you a—"

Bam! Bam! Bam! I smacked him over the head three times with the pistol, then grabbed him around the neck with my good arm and pulled him off my mother.

"Uhh. Uhh. What is going on? I just—" he started.

I straddled him and turned the gun upside down so that I was holding the barrel. *Bam! Bam! Bam! Bam! Bam!* "Bitch ass nigga! You don't put yo' hands on my mother!" *Bam! Bam! Bam!* The handle connected with his forehead again and again, opening him up.

Blood poured out of his face and I didn't give no fuck. I didn't care about him. Never had. Even after he and his wife, that he was now beating, adopted me, and kept me from being lost in the system. I never loved him. I only loved my mother, and I didn't know why that was, but that was just the facts.

"Shemar! Shemar! Holy fuck, bro! You're killing him! Please don't! I don't want you to go to jail!" Simone got up and started to pull me off his ass by my injured shoulder.

"Awww, fuck! Simone! I'm shot! You can't be doing that shit!" I winced in pain.

Purity ran over to us. "Get the fuck off my brother, bitch. He stoppin' yo' no good father from killin' yo' mother!"

They fell to the ground with Purity on Simone's back. Under me, the Pastor started to shake as if he was having a seizure. His face was a bloody mess. He coughed up a bloody loogey. I watched it bubble over his bottom lip and stay there. His eyes were closed, and I didn't know what to do with him next. Had the girls not been there, I would have killed him with two shots to the dome.

Instead of sending him on his way, I smacked him as hard as I can, jarring him awake. "Get yo' punk ass up and get out of here! Now!" I ordered, standing up and looking down on him. Behind me, the girls continued to wrestle and roll around on the floor. "Y'all, stop that shit!" I commanded as I leaned down and separated them.

Purity's chest heaved and so did Simone's. The girls did not like each other, and it was all because of me. I was sleeping with both.

The Pastor slowly got to his feet, then stumbled and fell against the wall with a thick rope of blood pouring from his mouth. He fell to one knee and tried to get back up, then fell again.

I kneeled and grabbed him up by his throat, helping him to his feet. The pain killers were not taking full effect. Wrapping one of his arms around my shoulder, I lead him through the house and out of the back door. We bumped into each other as I helped him to walk into the alley, before taking his arm from around my shoulder and throwing him into the green garbage cans back there. He fell over them loudly, causing a cat to shoot out from behind them and run down the alley with a huge rat in its mouth.

He opened his eyes and tried to say something, but no words came out, only more blood.

I kneeled and stuffed the barrel of my .9 down his throat. "You listen here, and you listen good. This is my family now. If you ever come near anyone of those females again, I'm gon' kill you. Do you hear me? I'm gon' blow yo' muthafuckin' brains out of yo' head like I should do right now. You's a coward. Only a coward would put his hands on a woman. The only reason I'm giving you a pass is because of Simone. Be thankful for that, because it will never happen again. Do you hear me? Nod yo' head if you do?"

He slowly nodded with his eyes wide open. They rolled to the back of his head more than once.

I stood up as a sharp pain shot through my shoulder. I noticed the whole left side of my shirt was drenched in my own blood. I felt dizzy and woozy. I staggered on my feet and made my way into the house.

When I got inside, Simone was washing our mother's face with a warm rag. My mother's head had swelled to twice its normal size. Both of her eyes were stuck closed from being punched so much. I remembered feeling the tears leaving my eyes as I looked her over. I felt like I had failed her, and that she would never look at me the same again. Though she was not my biological mother, she had been the only true mother I had ever known since I'd been alive. My biological mother had passed away from a drug overdose when I was just nine years old, but even before then, she had never been much of a mother to me and my sister Purity.

"Simone, get momma keys and take her to the hospital. Purity, you comin' with me. My nigga finna pick me and you up in like twenty minutes. I gotta go get this bullet out of me before I bleed out." While saying this, I was texting Taurus. I got so woozy that I passed out.

When I woke up, I was in the hospital with Purity sitting to the right of me. The room was spinning so bad that I didn't have any other choice but to go back to sleep, so it's what I did.

Chapter 2

I laid in that hospital bed for two days, then Taurus had all of us moved to his mansion out in Dallas. There, I was able to lean back while some of the finest women that I had ever seen in my life waited on me hand and foot for the next month. It got to the point where I was feeling strong enough to get out of the bed and back on my grind, but I neglected to, simply 'cuz Taurus had me feeling like a Don. One thing I could say for certain is that Purity didn't like seeing all of them broads fawn all over me. I mean, they gave me sponge baths and fed me my food one bite at a time, before wiping my mouth with a napkin, even when I didn't need them to. I got massages, and foot rubs, and even had one chick specifically hold my dick for me while I pissed.

I knew for a fact that it was the life that I was destined to live. I needed it more than my next breath and I knew I would do anything to get it. I couldn't see myself as a commoner. A regular hustler in the hood. I need to be filthy rich. I'm talking the kind where my family would never have to need or want for anything. I looked around the mansion and grew envious. I wanted everything that I saw, and more. Taurus was my key to the streets and I needed to find out how to make him beneficial to my long-term game plan. I deserved the life that he lived, and I had to have it.

Purity came into the big bedroom and plopped down on the bed next to me as the Asian and Black, half naked masseuse rubbed my back while I laid on my stomach. "Does that feel good, Shemar, or would you like for me to apply a little more pressure?" she asked with her lips against my ear.

I could feel her titties rubbing against my back. It made my dick hard. Her scent was Chanel. I wanted some of her. I had never had an Asian and Black chick before, and I was finding myself hella intrigued about what that would be like. She licked my earlobe before sucking on it.

I moaned a lil' bit and turned my face to look at her. Her big nipples stood at attention on her small breasts that couldn't have been more than a nice B cup. Before I could let her know how I was feeling, Purity spoke up.

"Can you give me and my brother a minute to talk, and come back and finish his massage later? I got something real important I want to run by him." She stood up and walked over to my masseuse, giving her a look that said she wasn't really asking but demanding her to leave.

The Asian and Black chick took a step back and looked Purity up and down, before smiling and licking her lips. "Taurus said that I belong to him until he dismisses me. So, for me to stop his massage or leave this room, he's going to have to tell me that." She looked Purity up and down one more time, then looked down to me with a wicked look on her face.

We made eye contact for a long time. Purity must've peeped it because she balled up her face, then walked into the Asian and Black chick's face. "Look, I don't give a fuck what Taurus told you. This my brother, right here, and I gotta talk to him, so you gotta leave. Besides, he don't need you to give him no massages. He got me for that. So, step off." She pressed her forehead to hers, clenching her jaw off and on.

The Asian and Black chick took a step back and laughed. "Damn, it's like that, Shemar?" She crossed her arms over her breasts, looking Purity in the eyes.

Purity stepped back into her face. "It's just like that. Step!"

By the time I sat up in the bed, the Asian and Black chick was on her way out of the room, shaking her head. "I still belong to you, Shemar, so just let me know when you need me, and I'll come running. From what I'm hearing, you supposed to be the next big thing out in Houston. You gon' get to know me real well. Trust me when I tell you that." She stepped out of the door with her purple, laced boy shorts all up in her thick ass cheeks. Her long hair fell to the middle of her back.

Purity stuck her face in front of mine and obstructed my view. "Damn, fuck that girl. You don't even need to be looking at her no way when I'm right here. Do you have any idea how that makes me feel?" She got up and closed the door, locking it, before sitting back on the bed beside me.

I flipped over to my back, feeling renewed from my thirty-minute massage. "Purity, you know it ain't even like that. Taurus just got so many broads walking around this mansion that I can't help but to peep most of them. These hoes bad; you gotta admit that." I grabbed my boxers from under the pillow and was getting ready to slide them on when Purity grabbed my wrist and stopped me.

"Wait a minute, Shemar, damn. Don't do that just yet." She pulled back my covers, exposing my nakedness. Then, she took her small hand and grabbed my dick to stroke it. Afterward, she leaned in and kissed the head. "I been feening for some of this. We been here a whole three weeks and ain't did nothin'. I'm so horny that I'm going crazy. I need you to fuck me, Shemar, right now."

She sucked my dick into her mouth, slurping my pole while I closed my eyes for a minute and enjoyed what she was putting down. Her tongue ran around my head, then she popped me out of her mouth and rub me against her cheek. "I love this dick so much, Shemar. I wish I never had to share it." Then, she started to suck me like an animal, making crazy noises that drove me absolutely insane.

I opened my eyes and saw that her skirt was up and around her waist. Her ass was bare, and her thighs were spread wide, putting that fat kitty on blast. I reached over her back and squeezed her ass, before sliding my hand in between her legs, playing with her wet pussy, slipping two fingers deep into her center.

"Huh. Huh. Huh. Huh." She sucked me faster and faster, and only stopped to pop me out of her mouth. "You don't need nobody but me, Shemar. I'll do whatever you want me to do. You know that." Then, she popped me back in and really got to going to town, slurping super loud.

My eyes rolled into the back of my head more than a few times. It was feeling so good that I started humping off the bed to go deeper. When I felt her nip my head with her teeth it was more than I could take. My abs tensed, and then I started to cum hard. "Shit, Purity. I'm cumming, ma. Fuck!"

She took my dick into her small fist, milking me for all that I was worth— sucking and forcing my seed out of me. The harder she tugged on him, the more I came until I had to remove her hand from my pipe.

I got up and threw her on her stomach, pushing her right leg to her ribs, sticking my face between her legs, then sucking her pussy lips into my mouth, spreading them, and trapping her big clit with my lips, running my tongue back and forth across it.

"Unnnn-a. Yes, Shemar! Ooooo-a. I love when you do me like this. You eat me so good." She got on her knees and put her face into the bed, whimpering.

I licked up and down her crease, sticking my tongue past her folds while I attacked her clit and sucked on her pussy lips like an animal. Her juices on my tongue made me looney. It sent chills through my bones. Every time I ate her, or we did anything forbidden, it made me feel that way. I had an evil bug in me that I couldn't control.

"Unn-a. Unn-a. Unn-a. I'm cumming, Shemar. Oooo-shit. I'm cumming, big bruh. It feels so goooood-a! Uhhh-shitttt!" She screamed and forced her ass back into my face while I attacked her clit like a savage until she released her juices all over my lips and tongue.

I jumped onto my knees and got behind her, took my dick and slid him deep into her middle, before pulling her back into me by her hips, hard, again and again. The pussy was gripping at me, causing me to groan in delight.

"Mmm. Mmm. Mmm. Mmm! Uh! Shit. Yes. Unn! Harder, Shemar! Uh! Uh! Uh! Uh! Uh! Mmm!

Ooo! Shit! Yes! I love it!" She smashed her ass back into me. I watched it wobble and shake. My dick went in and out of her juicy pussy repeatedly. Our scents filled the air, further driving me insane. "Grab my titties, Shemar, like you always do." She sounded out of breath. "Please. Grab. My titties. Uhhhhh-shit! I'm cummiiiing!"

I reached under her and grabbed a hold of both of her swinging breasts, pulling on the nipples while I banged into her at full speed, still watching the way my dick opened her up. Her sex lips sucked at me while her juices ran out of her. I knew I wouldn't be able to hold on much longer. It was becoming too much for me. Every time I hit her pussy, it always made me feel highly aroused for some reason. I gripped her hips as I felt her walls vibrating while she came. The feel of that was all it took to send me over the edge.

She smashed back into me with all her might, and I couldn't take it no more. "Cum in me, Shemar! Please!" She begged, slamming back into me harder and harder with her mouth wide open. Her nipples brushed against the sheet of the bed while little beads of sweat formed on her yellow back.

Wham. Wham. Wham. Wham. Wham. Then I was cumming deep within her channel.

Afterwards, we would lay with her on my chest, kissing it, before looking up at me for a long time without saying anything. "Shemar, I love you so much. I hope you know that." She rubbed my stomach muscles, then kissed me on the chest.

I rubbed all over her soft booty. Then, I took my finger and ran it along her hot crack, all the way down to her pussy. Both lips were engorged and a little open. "I love you too, baby. You know I'd do anything for you. You're my world, Purity." I leaned down and kissed her on the forehead.

She lifted, exposing her titties, kissing me on the lips, sucking on them, and moaning into my mouth. "Mmm. I love kissing you. It drives me insane, because how many girls get to do what I'm doing right now?" She kissed me again, then laid her head in the crux of my neck while I continued to rub all over that fat ass booty. Her scent was heavy in the air and I loved it. "Shemar, I got somethin' that I want to tell you, but I don't want you to be mad at me." She rubbed my chest, rolling her thumb around my nipple.

I closed my eyes because I felt a little tired. I was supposed to have a large dinner with Taurus and his wife that night, but I was feeling like I wanted to cancel it. Digging all in Purity's body had me depleted. I felt like I needed a nap or something. "What's the matter, Purity? You already know you can tell me anything."

She looked up at me and kissed me on the cheek, then leaned down and kissed my stomach again. "I got rid of that baby." She looked up at me with a scared look on her face. "About two weeks after I moved in with you and the Pastor's wife, I had your foster mother, Vicki, take me down and get that situation taken care of. I couldn't go through with having another man's baby growing inside of me. It wouldn't have been from me and you, and I could have never loved it, no matter what." She grabbed my face between her little hands. "Are you mad at me? Be honest, too."

I sat up in the bed and looked directly at her. I wasn't mad. I mean, most women would have probably gotten rid of a baby that was placed inside of them by rape. You see, the Deacon of our old church and his son had been raping Purity ever since they adopted her into their family. My sister didn't know exactly whose baby it was. It was because of their raping her that I wound up putting their asses six feet under. Had it been up to me, they would have been buried deeper than that.

I leaned forward and kissed her lips. "N'all. I'm not mad. I told you back when I found out that that decision was up to you. So, you made it and I stand by you one hundred percent." I wrapped her into my arms, pulled her naked body on top of mine, and slid down into the bed.

"Shemar, can I be honest with you about something?" she asked, rubbing my stomach, and putting her thick thigh across me.

I could feel her hot pussy on my hip. "Yeah, baby, go ahead. After this, we finna take a nap or somethin', awright?" I placed my hand on to the small of her back, then ran it down to that ass again. I couldn't help it, she was so strapped.

"That's cool. I'm tired too. What I wanted to say was that I don't want Simone to have your baby because its gon' make you love her more than me. Now I know you gon' say that it ain't, but I already know that it is, because that's how the game go. Now, am I wrong?" She raised her head up a lil' bit so she could look me in the face.

I yawned and smacked my lips together. I was so tired. I really didn't want to get into one of those discussions with Purity because, no matter what I told her during these times, she never felt like I was seeing the bigger picture. She always felt that one day somebody would steal my love away from her, for one reason or the other, and I knew for a fact that I would never allow anything like that to happen. Purity was my life. We'd been all that we'd had ever since she was born.

I looked down at her and smiled, leaning my head forward to kiss her on the forehead. She closed her eyes and melted under my lips as she often did at any affection that I showed her. "I hear what you saying, lil' momma, but she's already pregnant, and I must stand as a man and take care of my responsibility. As far as me loving her more than you, that will never happen. You will always be first in my life, and I been telling you that ever since you were old enough to understand what I was saying."

She looked me over for a long time, then laid her head in the crux of my neck. "So, even when she has the baby, you're telling me that you aren't going to want to build a family with her and leave me all alone? I'm telling you now, Shemar, that I could not survive that. I wanna be with you for the rest of my life. I hope you know that I'm not playin' when I say that." She raised her head and looked into my face again. "Well, do you?"

I closed my eyes and pulled her back down to my chest. "Purity, you stressin' yourself out over nothin'. I got you, boo. I'll never let you go either, no matter what takes place in life. I promise."

"And the family thing, what about that? Can you see yourself having a family with her one day? You know, doing the whole marriage thing? Can you see her being your wife? 'Cuz if you can, I see myself killing her with one of your guns. Ain't nobody gon' take you away from me, Shemar. I'll be everything that you need and then some. You don't need no other woman outside of me. I swear you don't." She straddled me then laid her head on my chest. I could feel her sex lips smashed up against my lower stomach.

I wrapped my arms around her and we fell asleep, just like that.

Chapter 3

Nikki knocked on the door, three days later, looking for me after not seeing me the whole time because I had been held up in the room with Purity. For seventy-two hours straight, we were laying up and doing everything sexual that we could think of. Occasionally, Taurus would have the Asian and Black chick come through and she would give me a sponge bath while Purity went off and took a shower or got us something to eat.

I found out that her name was Eve, and every time Purity was out of ear shot, she did her best to come at me, saying shit like: "Damn, what y'all doing is hot. If she didn't have so much of an attitude, I would love to be in the middle of you two, because I love that forbidden shit. You should ask her if I can join y'all. I promise she won't regret it." That's what Eve figured, but as soon as I brought it up to Purity, she damn near bit my head off.

So, Nikki beat on the bedroom door three days later, right after me and Purity got done doing our thing. I slipped into my boxers and went and answered the door, while Purity looked on in anger, figuring that it was about to be Eve. Once she saw that it was Nikki, she rolled over and dozed off.

"Damn, Shemar, you ain't left the room in three days. You need to give Purity lil' pussy a rest. She ain't ready for all that just yet," she joked, then stepped past me.

I closed the door behind her and locked it, following her over to the bed where she took a seat on the side that I was sleeping on. "How them wounds doing?" I asked, refusing to make eye contact with her.

It wasn't that I was ashamed at what me and Purity was doing. I just couldn't look her in the eye for a minute because I still had not confirmed or denied that I had been in there fucking her for three days straight.

She shrugged. "I'm good. I been tooting Oxys all day, and I can't feel shit. This morning, when I woke up, I was a lil' sore, but I'm healing just right." She looked over to Purity's lying form in the bed and put her hand on Purity's ass, which was under the sheets. "She got a big booty," she whispered, shaking her head. Then, she sniffed the air. "It don't smell like nothin' but sex in here. Y'all been getting it in." She rubbed Purity's ass some more, watching her hand coast over her globes.

I sat on the bed, then laid back with my head on the pillow. To be honest, I kind of liked watching her rub all over Purity. That shit was a turn on. Purity opened her eyes and snuggled against me. She looked down and saw that it was Nikki rubbing her booty, jerked her head to look back and me, then smiled, laying her head onto my chest while Nikki continued.

"Taurus say we on business today. He wanted me to get you up before he flew in from Miami. He say he got some business that he need you to handle for him, out that way." She snaked her hand under the cover and moved Purity's thighs apart while she laid on her stomach. Then, I saw her hand go between her legs and get to moving back and forth at a steady pace.

Purity moaned. "Mmm-a. Fuck, Nikki. Ummm-a." She opened her legs wider and kissed my chest with her eyes closed.

Nikki continued to play with her, smiling, and licking her lips. "I knew her pussy was fat. You can tell by the way she walk. But, anyway." She took her hand from under the sheet and sucked her fingers. "Taurus told me to tell you that y'all gon' be flyin out this afternoon, and to be ready in an hour." She got off the bed and wagged her finger in my face. "So, no more fucking for the time being. I know it's hard to stay off her lil' fine ass, but you got business to take care of. We still gotta get our piece of Cloverland and smash Vito punk ass for doing this to us. You are still the head of our destiny, so let's make it happen. I love you, Shemar." She kissed me on the lips and I could taste and smell purity's pussy all over her mouth.

Ninety minutes later, I had explained to Purity that I would be back, and that she didn't have to tag along with me everywhere. I found myself sitting in the second row of Hood Rich's private jet, across from Taurus who leaned his head down and tooted up a thin line of cocaine, before pulling on his nose. He picked up the bottle of Moet and drank out of it.

"Awright, now look, Shemar. I know that whole thing with Vito didn't go down the way that it was supposed to, and we gon' rectify that, but for now, we gotta move on to the next mission. I'm taking you down here to Miami with me, so you can knock this nigga head off and make a statement. I don't want to go too far into why you doing what you doing because the less you know the better. What I can tell

31

you is that this punk thinks he finna make his way out to Houston to corner the drug market, not knowing that we already got that shit cornered." He leaned down and tooted up two more lines, then went into his pocket and handed me a bottle of Oxys.

My eyes lit up as I grabbed them from him, poured two on the metal plate that he gave me before crushing them up, and separating them into two lines. Ever since I had gotten shot, I would feel pain shooting all over me. Those pills were the only remedy for that. They made me feel pain-free and like I could do anything. I snorted the pills, took the bottle from Taurus, and drank from it, already feeling the effects coursing through me. Immediately my body felt numb and mellow. I smiled.

I sipped the Moet and looked across at Taurus. "I'm down for whatever, man, just as long as somewhere down the line I get to handle my business on that nigga Vito. I can't take what he did to my people." I passed him back the bottle.

Hood Rich came from the front of the plane and sat in the seat next to mine. "Just focus on one mission at a time, lil' homie. It's dangerous to think ahead to your next mission before you handle the one that's in front of you. You have my word that you gone get yo' chance to get at Vito. It's already somethin' in the works as we speak, but for now, you going to Miami to hit this Haitian cat named Pony. You have to cut this snake off at the head before he moves in our direction. We'll be going to a party tonight that one of my club promoters are throwing. Pony will be there. We'll make sure that you and him are isolated, and as soon as you are, you will have less than five minutes to do what you need to do because he has an army of killas that look out for him," Hood Rich said, pouring cocaine out on the tray, then taking his pinky nail and tooting it that way.

Taurus drank from the Moet again. "After you handle this business, Shemar, I wanna get you situated out in Cloverland with the Rebirth. I wanna see you rich like us. I wanna watch you shine. You hear me?"

I most definitely did, and I was ready to take my place in the game. I didn't care what I had to do. The name of the club was Dollas. When we pulled up in front of it, in a stretch Navigator, there had to be about fifty people waiting outside to get into it. Hood Rich stepped out of the limo first, followed by Taurus and then me. I was dressed in an all-black and red Michael Kors fit, with the Versace shades, and a hundred thousand-dollar Rolex that Hood Rich had given me before we set out for the club. That boy was iced in black diamonds and had a red face. I had twenty thousand dollars on me that Hood Rich said was to be used for the strippers.

He wanted me to use every penny of it on them, so instead of getting it all in ones, I got it in fives. I felt like that would make more of a statement until Taurus said that he would be throwing twenties.

When we stepped out of the truck, we had to walk alongside of the line of people that were waiting to get inside. They gave us some crazy looks as we walked to the front like we didn't have a care in the world.

Once there, a big beefy, bald white dude with an ear piece looked us over with anger. "Back of the line, gentlemen." He snarled.

Taurus smiled and shook his head. "N'all that back of the line shit is for normal people, not bosses." He pulled out a knot of hundreds and handed it to the security man. "That's just for you. I know this profession don't make no money. Other than that, if you check yo' list, we're on it. My name is Taurus, this Hood Rich, and this is our plus one. Name not needed. In fact, that's what it should say once you look us up." He put his arm around me and laughed. "This that boss shit that you gotta get used to, Shemar. Fuck this world. Make this muhfucka suck yo' dick once you get yo' chips up. You understand me?"

I nodded and looked over the line behind us. It had a few bad lil' broads that I would have loved to get to know.

The security dude pulled out a tablet and went over it, before shaking his head. "Here you are, put down as a special guest. VIP and everything." He removed the velvet rope. "Please enjoy yourself at our establishment." He took a stamper and stamped our hands before admitting us into the club.

As soon as we came through the door, we were met by two big ass white dudes that stood by a metal detector. They looked like police officers of some sort. Behind them I could hear the music coming out of the club. They had on a Cardi B number. I nodded and watched Hood Rich clear the metal detector, then Taurus. I went last. I knew I was good because Taurus had told me not to bring any weapons for this job. Everything I needed would be supplied to me inside of the club.

I walked through the metal detector and into the next area, which was the coat check. We gave them our light jackets and stepped past another velvet rope. A Brazilian chick, who was about five feet three inches tall, wore a Prada body suit that was so tight it showcased everything that she had under it. She stepped forward with a black light, running it over our stamps. At seeing that we were VIP, she smiled. I peeped her hug Taurus and slipping him something that I couldn't make out. He put it into the small of his back and kissed her on the cheek.

She turned around and waved her hand through the air. I saw another Brazilian chick just as fine and thick come through the crowd, holding a tray of drinks in her hand. The first one let her know what our situation was. "Hey, these guys are VIP customers. Make sure you put them in the Mezzanine section, right by the stage. Take good care of them." At saying this, she winked at Taurus.

The second chick nodded and looked us over as if she were hungry or something. "You guys follow me. I'll make sure that you're taken care of." She pushed a button on the side of her tray and it lit up green, then we made our way through the dancing crowd of people.

To my right, there were two stages with strippers on them, doing the most. One had a black female who was twerking like her life depended on it, while the other one had a Spanish female who slid down her pole, got to the bottom, bent over and pressed her bald pussy against it, separating her folds. I damn near bumped into a few people looking at all of that.

To my left were three bars that were under different colors of lights. They were packed, and the bar tenders threw bottles of liquor up in the air, catching them, then poured the liquor into the waiting patron's glasses. More than once females passed by us and smiled, after looking us up and down hungrily

One chick bumped into me and licked her lips. "You wanna go home with me?" She asked, then grabbed my dick. Even though she was bad as hell, probably Puerto Rican or something, I had to turn her down and keep my mind focused on the task at hand.

It seemed like it took us ten minutes to make it to our Mezzanine seats, but once we got there, it was already two bottles of Moet waiting for us on ice, and a bottle of Moscato. The seats were all leather and situated in the form of a U. It looked like a partial glass cubicle, sectioned off for our own privacy, I imagined. To top it off, we were less than twenty feet away from the main stage. The stripper had to walk past our section to get onto the stage. I liked that set up immediately.

I sat back and popped the champagne as a dancer walked past us and headed to the main stage. She was caramel skinned with a big ass booty that jiggled as she walked up the stairs. She looked over her shoulder at us and smiled before a musical number by Jhene Aiko started, and she got to doing her thing. She walked around the pole, gyrating her hips against it, dropping to her knees and backing her ass all the way up so that the pole went in between her ass cheeks while she rubbed them up and down it.

Taurus leaned into my ear. "Shemar, take yo' paper and start making it rain on that lil' bitch. You see to yo' left up there, in that VIP box?" He pointed in the direction he wanted me to look at with his head.

I looked to my left and saw about five niggas, well dressed in Burberry, with plenty gold jewelry on, who had their eyes on the stage. "Yeah, I see them. What about 'em?" I asked, sizing them up really good. Even from the distance, I could see that they had plenty champagne bottles on their table and a pile of money.

"That's that nigga Pony crew right there. He the one that's sittin' back with the bottle in his hand. You see?"

I nodded. I could see the dark-skinned dude with the Boosie fade. He had some diamonds on his fingers that glistened from afar. "Yeah, I see him."

"Yeah, well, that's the nigga you finna kill. He want the streets that I'm giving you, Shemar. This nigga wanna come from Haiti and take over what's rightfully yours. He ain't bled on yo' streets. That nigga don't know what it feels like to go to war over them streets. All he cares about is capitalizing off what we already worked so hard to build. Houston is yours, Shemar, because you were bred by those slums; not that fuck nigga. So, you gotta knock his ass off to reach yo' King Pin status. You got that? Let me go set this shit up, I'll be back. Just make it rain on that bitch out there. Make a scene because that's important." He got up and made his way through the crowd of people.

Hood Rich slid his gloves in place. Instead of following Taurus, he went in the opposite direction. I didn't know what he was up to, but I was gon' follow the orders that Taurus had given me. I unzipped the green bag that held my $20,000 worth of five-dollar bills, taking the money out in a bundle and heading to the main stage with it.

The sistah up there was making her ass clap while she laid on her stomach. She pulled her G string to the side to expose her sex lips, slid a finger though them and sucked on her bottom lip all sexy like. She had my full attention.

I took a about two hundred dollars and threw it in the air, causing it to rain down on her in slow motion. She crawled on her knees into the shower, pointed her ass at me and shook while I put another bundle in my hand and fanned the cash at her over and over again. This caused another stripper to run on stage. She was dark-skinned and super strapped, but with way too much make up. She hit the splits in front of me, and looked over her shoulder, licking her lips while her naked pussy bounced up and down. I took some more money and threw it all the way up in the air.

I looked to my left and some of the dudes that Taurus had me peep earlier were digging into a bag. They mugged me, then sucked their teeth. Not to be out done by me, they took handfuls of money and tossed it into the air over the strippers. I saw the bills were all ones, but they were throwing so much that I guessed by the end of their display it would add up to way over $20,000.

A green siren started to go off and more and more strippers ran out and onto the stage. They were shaking their asses and popping their pussies while we made it thunderstorm with cash. I looked to my left again and now it seemed like eight of Pony's men were out there throwing cash into the air. They did all they could to outdo me as more and more strippers came onto the stage and got down and dirty.

Hood Rich came beside me and leaned down. "I'll take it from here. You know where we came in at right?" He nodded to the front of the club as the Deejay tried to hype up the ballers in the club to compete with each other and throw more money.

"This how we can tell is eating out in these Miami streets! This is where you build yo' name from. Let's make it rain baby! Coo-we!" he shouted.

Now Pony's crew was throwing $5 bills. The stage looked like the strippers were dancing in a bank vault. More strippers invaded the section and started to bum rush Pony's men by putting their asses in their laps, and dancing all over them.

I nodded at Hood Rich. "Yeah, I remember where we checked our coats in at. Why? What's good?"

Two Chainz's "Man, I Love Dem Strippers" sounded in the speakers, causing the dancers to go crazy with excitement. There was so much ass shaking jumping off that I felt like I had ADD. I couldn't focus the way I was supposed to.

"You are to meet Taurus there right now. Go!" He opened his bag of money and threw it at the dancers that were all around Pony's men. This caused pandemonium.

I made my way through the crowd as fast as I could. People were headed around the main stage which meant I bumped into a lot of people on my way in the opposite direction. Quite a few women grabbed my arm and tried to pull me along with them. It was crazy to say the least.

When I got to the front of the club where we'd checked in our jackets, the female from before that Taurus had hugged and she'd slipped him something, stepped into my path. "Hey! Taurus told me you were coming. Follow me. Hurry up!" She grabbed my hand and took me through a door that was about ten feet away from where we'd checked our coats in. Once we stepped through the door, we entered a hallway with red carpet and gold trim. "Come on, he's back here."

I felt my heart thumping in my chest as I was being led by this fine ass female who had her G string deep within the crack of her ass. With every step that she took, her ass would jiggle along with her thick thighs. I had to shake my head with all my might to get out of the zone that her body was placing me in. Finally, we got to the end of the hallway and stopped outside of a door that was marked as private.

She turned around to look at me. "Okay, you're on your own from here. Handle your business and tell Taurus I'll meet him at the Bellagio at three. Good luck." She knocked on the door three times, then jogged down the hall, disappearing.

The door opened and my eyes damn dear jumped out of my head.

Chapter 4

Taurus had Pony up against the wall with his big hand around his neck. "Close that door, Shemar, and come over here and handle this business."

I did just what he asked, then turned back to look at what was before me. Pony kicked his legs wildly while Taurus held him with a forearm under his chin. From a distance, Pony had looked like a big dude, but now that I was seeing him up close, I peeped that he was real skinny and just full of jewelry.

Taurus put his face close to his. "You bitch ass nigga, you thought it was sweet. I told you, you was dealing with some new jacks to this shit. All yo' niggas down there chasing pussy while you up here in a sticky situation. Shoulda stayed yo' ass in Haiti like Hood Rich told you, my nigga. Now its curtains." Taurus reached into the small of his back and came up with a Kitana Blade. It looked like a knife you would slit the throat of deer with after you shot them. He handed it to me while Pony struggled against him. "Murk this nigga, Shemar. Take yo' throne, lil' homie."

I took the blade and scrunched my face, wrapping my hand around the handle. With my left hand, I moved Taurus out of the way a little bit, so I could aim for Pony's stomach. As soon as that path was clear, I cocked my arm back and lunged the knife forward, implanting it into his stomach deeply.

"Ugggghhh!" He hollered and hunched over.

This made Taurus stand to the side with a big smile on his face. "Kill 'em, Shemar. You my lil' nigga. You ride under me. Fuck this Haitian punk. He thought it was sweet."

I pulled the knife out and slammed it back into Pony's stomach again, this time trying to pick him up with the handle. He stepped on to his tippy toes with his eyes wide open and coughed up blood, before rushing me with all the might he had left. We fell to the carpet with the knife still deep within him.

"Ughhh! Ughhh!" He swung and bussed me in the jaw, causing my head to snap real hard to the left.

Bam! Taurus kicked him so hard in the face that he flew backward. "Get yo punk ass off my lil' nigga!" He roared.

As soon as he was on his back, I jumped up and straddled him, raising the knife in the air and bringing it down with all my might into his chest, again and again, while my face stung from his blow.

After I'd hit him up like ten times, Taurus reached down and put a finger to his throat, checking for a pulse. Once he confirmed that Pony was dead, he stood up and took the knife away from me, wiping the blood on Pony's clothes, cleaning the handle then dropping it on to the carpet before we made our way out of that club.

Back on the jet, I gave Taurus the message that the stripper had given me about meeting him at the Bellagio.

He nodded his. "Good looking, lil' homie." He smiled and grabbed a bottle of Moet out of the small refrigerator, handing me one. "You don't have any idea what we just did do you?"

I shook my head as I looked out at the dark clouds that were floating around the plane. I was interested to see what he was about to say next. I hoped I didn't fail some kind of test or something.

"By killing Pony, we just waged war with the Zo Pound Mafia out of the Port. You see, their King sent a message to me and Hood Rich that he was sending Pony to take over Houston, and it would be in our best interest to step to the side or a war would be waged. Their King's name is Yohan, and Pony was his nephew." Taurus closed his eyes and sipped out of the Moet with a smile on his face.

Hood Rich sat across from me, eating barbecue chicken. "You see, muhfuckas think that just because we got millions, Shemar, that we don't get down no more. But when you get up here where we're at, you got to get even more grimier because it's no longer about blocks and hoods. It's about whole states, and regions of the country. The Zo Pound Mafia is huge internationally and are looking to step foot into the United States, which is our turf. Shit can't happen like that." He bit into a drumstick and ripped the meat from the bone.

Taurus took a long swallow from the bottle of Moet and burped. "You getting a first-hand lesson on how the game goes, once you make it out of the hood. Only bitch niggas hide behind their money and don't get their hands dirty. We ain't them. We were bred by the slums and we gon' continue to dominate the game in a bloody fashion. It's the only life I know. I don't give a fuck if I had a billion dollars. I know how to make a muhfucka bow down to my gangsta." He turned the bottle all the way up.

Hood Rich sucked his fingers and grabbed a piece of bread, chewing on it. "After you kill Vito tomorrow at his daughter's christening, Cloverland is yours, and we gon' help you flood it with the Rebirth. I wanna see some M's in yo' bank account, lil nigga, because that's what you deserve for yo' people. You taking care of a lot of women out there, and they are expensive. That's the first lesson I want you to learn. You gotta make sure that the women in your life are well taken care of, because when it all falls, they are going to be the ones that will hold you together if you so happen to go on the inside. Loyalty with men only last but so long, the female version of loyalty is embedded within her heart first, and then her brain. You take care of them the right way and you'll never have to worry about hitting rock bottom. Trust me." He bit into another drum stick and went to town on it.

I heard everything that he said, and I was agreeing with him one hundred percent. I had always been the one to put the females in my life first even before myself. I was just built that way. I would do anything for either one of the women in my life that I really loved and cared about.

"What's good with this christening? When am I doing this?" I asked Taurus who was taking a barbecued breast of chicken out of the metal bowl and placing it on his plate.

He sucked his thumb and smiled. "Oh, we found out that Vito is having his daughter's christening out in San Antonio. From there, he gon' be shacked up with one of our hoes. We could be bogus and kill him in the church in front of all his people, or we can wait and hit his ass back at the Hilton after he send his baby mother and kids back to Houston. If you asked me, I really don't give a fuck. I ain't got no love for that, after he how he tried to get down on me a few weeks back," Taurus said, tearing the skin from his chicken and popping it into his mouth, chewing. "Only reason I ain't been kilt that nigga is because of Blaze. I got a lot of love for lil' momma, but it's only so much I can accept while I'm in this game, and I've accepted more from him and his branch of our business than anybody ever in my life." He closed his eyes and dunked a piece of bread into the barbecue sauce that was on his plate before tossing it into his mouth and chewing while shaking his head. "Damn, shawty put her foot in this chicken," he said with a mouthful of food. It sounded like he was talking with his thumb in his mouth.

I couldn't take it no more. Seeing them go to work on that food like that made me hungry. I grabbed me a thigh and bit into it like a savage, spilling barbecue sauce all over Hood Rich's white carpet inside of his Jet. I didn't even care. I was pretty sure he would have it shampooed later or something. I chewed my food and swallowed, honestly seeing why they were enjoying it so much. It was seasoned to the tee, and the flavor was amazing. I shook my head just like Taurus was doing while he ate. "Well, no matter where y'all want me to hit him at, I'm all for it. I'm ready to go on to the next phase, so if I gotta crush this nigga, then just tell me how you want it done and when." I bit into my chicken again, with my eyes rolling into the back of my head. I ain't exaggerating, it was that damn good.

Taurus nodded. "Well, let me figure out how I want you to do it, and I'll let you know. I'ma rollout there with you while Hood Rich get the Rebirth ready for mass distribution throughout Cloverland. After you murder this punk, it's time to get yo' bands all the way up. You can't begin to understand the game until you see what it feels like to be rich. Fuck with me and give me yo' loyalty and I'ma take you where you need to be. You feeling me right now?" Taurus asked, grabbing the bottle of Moet, getting ready to sip out of it. He looked me over closely.

I pulled a piece of white meat from the bone and popped it into my mouth after dunking it in the barbecue sauce that oozed off of the other portion of chicken. "Taurus, I pledge my loyalty to you, big homie, with everything that I am as a man. I'll never bite the hand that feeds me."

Hood Rich wiped his hands on a wet napkin and nodded before taking a blunt from behind his ear and lighting it, inhaling deeply. "I don't know what it is about you, Shemar, but I just see a thorough nigga when I look at you. It ain't no doubt in my mind that you gon' be a major player in this game out here. You just stay close to us and soak up every bit of game that you can. Let knowledge be your cup, and wisdom be the liquid that you drink, and you gon' be alright. Always strive to think four moves ahead in this game, or with everything in life, period. Work from ahead and never from behind. Analyze every person that ever steps in front of you, including us. Learn their strengths and weaknesses and capitalize off of both. The game is designed for you to advance when others fail. It's crazy, but it's fair. Most importantly, your heart must be as cold as ice. Any signs of weakness and you'll be eaten alive. You hear me?" Hood Rich asked, looking at me through his Ray Ban's.

I nodded. "Yeah, I hear you, big homie."

That night, I rolled out to the hospital so I could see my mother. Prior to that day, I had only been in contact with her through the use of phone, but I was missing her and I felt like I just needed to be in her physical presence. So, I rolled out with Nikki, all the way to Houston. I didn't bring Purity because I knew she would have gotten into an argument with Simone and I just didn't feel like going through that this day. I needed to be there for my mother— to console her and build her up in any way that she needed me to.

Nikki sat back in her seat and puffed on a blunt of Loud, nodding her head to the SZA track bellowing out of the speakers to Taurus' Bentley he'd let me use to get to Houston this night. She reached and turned down the system. "You know that nigga Taurus and his wife did a number on me last night." She shook her head. "Ummph. I thought I was falling in love with his fine ass until Princess bussed me all the way down and taught my pussy how to do some shit that I didn't even know she was capable of doing. I still got chills." She wrapped her arms around herself and shook in dramatic fashion.

I looked over at her and laughed. "Princess is fine as hell. I be trying my best to not look at her when she be walking through the crib wearing next to nothing. For her to be so small, she kinda strapped with it."

I had peeped her a few times and I was impressed with her lil' frame. She had this way about her that was real alluring. I kept hearing Taurus saying what

I would accomplish if I remained loyal to him, so I tried to push his wife's image out of my head; not that I would have went there with her no way, but I did find myself lusting after her like crazy. His daughter Jahliya was just as fine, but way thicker.

Nikki took a strong pull, then handed the blunt to me as I increased my speed on the highway. "Boy, you betta be careful. Purity catch yo' ass looking at her and she'll body Princess and you. You know she ain't going. She wants her brother all to herself. Simone just don't know what she up against." She laughed again and shook her head.

I smiled. "You just loving that shit, huh?" I took a pull of the blunt and inhaled deeply, feeling the smoke burn my chest. The high came over me right away, but it didn't stop me from taking four more quick pulls, and inhaling, holding the smoke.

Nikki grabbed the blunt back. "I'm just stating facts. That girl ain't playing about you. Y'all been forced to be separated for how long? Man, now that she able to be with you physically and y'all done the do, she'd rather die than let somebody else have you. I'm telling you this in a joking manner, but I'm serious as hell. So, what's yo' end game with her?"

I jerked my head back as I pulled around a slow driving ass semi-truck, switching lanes, and increasing my speed, trying to get to Houston as fast as possible. I shrugged. "I ain't really got no end game. I'm just living in the moment with my sister. I love her with all of my heart, and I'll do anything to heal her. She been through a lot. She felt like the only way I would be able to love her as much as I do Simone is if we laid down and did what we did. Now that we have, I really ain't got no regrets. I enjoyed that shit just as much as she did, so it is what it is."

Nikki turned more in her seat so she could face me better. "Shemar, don't tell me that you that damn stupid." She frowned in anger.

I continued to drive through the night. "What are you talking about?" I found myself confused.

She took a deep breath and exhaled. "Don't you know how girls work, or females, period? Bruh, the more you put yo' dick in that girl, the harder she's going to fall for you because you represent unconditional love to her, and that's something that she has never had outside of you. Due to the fact that she's been deprived of it for so long, now that she has it, not only in a mental capacity, but also a physical one from the most sacred and safest person in the world to her, she will never let it go. You're going to be all that she desires, so you have to have a game plan for when you release her for Simone, or whoever, she's going to be devastated. So, I'm going to ask you again, what is your end game with her, because you have to have one unless you're planning on being with her for the rest of y'all lives?" She rubbed my face with her soft, open palm. "Shit more difficult than you think. For you, it's just sex, but for her it's that plus everything that really matters beyond that."

I rode on silence for a long time, just playing over everything that she was saying. I really never looked that deep into me and Purity's relationship. I honestly thought I was just healing her for the moment. You know, being there for her until she was strong enough to rise up and stand on her own two feet. I already knew that I would do anything for her. I mean, I would die for my sister at the drop of a hat, with no hesitation. As far as her becoming attached to me, and me needing to have a game plan on how to release her, or venture off to somebody else, I think I would just cross that bridge when I came to it.

For now, I wanted to live in the moment. I enjoyed what we had, and as much as she needed me, I needed her just the same. I don't know if I would have ever admitted that to anyone out loud, but it was my truth. Physically, emotionally and mentally, Purity was my oasis. The only time I ever felt whole was when she and I were together. So, as much as Nikki swore that she was falling for me because of our act, I honestly was falling for her just as hard. I didn't know how to process that reality in my mind, and to be honest, I really didn't want to. I didn't care what society thought, and I still don't to this day. Purity was my everything, and I would do all that I could to be hers as well.

We must've rolled for twenty minutes before Nikki reached over and squeezed my thigh. "You okay, Shemar? You been real quiet. I hope I didn't say something that pissed you off. You know I'm just keeping shit one hundred with you."

I picked her hand up and kissed it. "You good, Nikki. If I can't get the cold, hard truth from you, then who else would I get it from?" I reached over and moved her hair out of her pretty face. "In regard to Purity, I think I'm good. The same way she feeling about me, I'm feeling about her. I know what I gotta do, and I know how much she needs me. I won't fail her. Our whole lives I never have. That's my baby."

I smiled and looked back out at the road. The hospital was only ten minutes away.

Nikki shook her head. "Damn! That girl so fuckin' lucky. I wish I had a brother like you that was crazy about me like you is about her. I wouldn't let no bitch fuck with him either. Y'all both lucky. I'd kill for some shit like that." She sat back in her seat and crossed her arms as if she were super jealous.

I had never seen that side of her. I reached over and slapped her playfully on her thick thigh, watching it jiggle. "Fuck is you talking about? I'm yo' brother and I love you like a muhfucka. It ain't nothin' in this world that I wouldn't do for you. You know that." I was getting a lil' annoyed because Nikki should have already known what it was when it came to her and me. We had been through way too much shit together.

She moved my hand off of her thigh aggressively, sitting up in her seat. "Tell me somethin', Shemar. Why haven't you and I ever fucked? Huh? What? Is there something wrong with me?" She looked like she was about to cry. Once again, I had never seen that side of her before.

I scrunched my face. "What are you talking about? Me and you ain't ever got down like that because you my right-hand man, and I respect you too much. Then, on top of that, all I ever seen you fuck with is hoes, up until recently. Where is this coming from?" I asked, looking her over closely and pulling into the hospital's lot.

She took a deep breath and exhaled slowly. "Look, I'm just wondering, because if you'll be there for Purity in that way, what's to stop you from healing me like that? There have been times where I needed you just as much as she does. I mean, you've been the only brother that I've known since forever. Do you understand how cold this world can be when a female doesn't have a man that's standing beside her, against all odds? I mean, for the longest you've been that for me, but now it's like I gotta divide you between Simone and Purity. I want you to myself. Not as my man or nothin', but just as my right hand, and I want that option to lay you down, too. Shit, I got needs that only pure love can fulfill, and I know you're the only one that has that for me." She blinked tears.

I turned off the ignition and grabbed her into my embrace, laying her head on my chest. "So, what are you saying Nikki, because you're confusing me right now. I need you to be clear and uncut. Please, ma."

She tried to talk but her voice cracked really badly. She cleared her throat and tried again. "I don't know, Shemar. I guess I'm just saying don't forget that I am a woman and that I have emotional needs that only you can fulfill. Sometimes, don't look at me as some rider beside you. See me as a woman that needs you to protect her, even when I can protect myself. It's nice to be saved every now and then, even when you are a savage like me."

I hugged her for a long time, listening to her cry against me. I could tell that she was broken. That her rough and tough exterior was not identical to her interior make-up. All the years that I had been riding beside Nikki, I had never looked at her as anything less of a beast than me, and I still didn't, but this is the night that I actually saw that underneath it all, my right-hand was all woman and needed me to respect her femininity.

"If ever, and however you need me, Nikki, just let me know and I am yours. I promise you this with all of my heart. I love you, and I see you for who you are. I appreciate that." I kissed her on the forehead and held her for a little while longer in silence.

Ghost

Chapter 5

I leaned over my mother as she opened her eyes in the hospital bed. They were still swollen; her face unrecognizable. The Pastor had done more than a number on her. It was almost impossible for me to look at her without wanting to break down in tears. She had adopted me when I was nine years old, and every day of my life, since then, she had done nothing less than given me all of herself. I loved her just like a mother, and I felt horrible for not being able to save her from that abusive man. I rubbed her hair out of her face, leaned down and kissed her bruised cheek softly.

She smiled as my image came into view clearly for her. She was hooked up to so many machines that I worried. "Mmm. Shemar. It's about time you got here, baby. I been missing you so bad." Her voice sounded loopy. I could tell that she was on morphine.

I laid my cheek against hers and rubbed her exposed arm. "How are you doing, my Queen?" Tears fell down my cheeks.

The machines continued to beep on the side of us. One of them sounded like it was inhaling and exhaling air loudly. I kissed my mother on the cheek and looked down on her, swallowing my spit while images of me killing the Pastor ran through my mind. I felt like I could cut him up into little pieces and eat his bitch ass throughout the day. I didn't know if I had that cannibal shit in me, but the way I was feeling in that moment, I felt like I could do anything vicious to him with a smile on my face. My mother was sacred to me; always had been. I rubbed her forehead.

"I'm okay, baby. Certain areas still hurt me really bad, but I'm functioning. I've been thinking a lot about you, though. I thought you were mad at me for some reason, which is why you haven't been to see me. I don't know what I would do if I failed my little man. You know I live for you." Her voice broke up. "I didn't mean to mess up, baby. I swear I didn't."

I don't know how it happened, but all of the strength went out of my legs and I fell beside her, holding on to her stomach. Just hearing her words took all of the fight out of me. I couldn't stop myself from breaking down. "Momma, never. Never have you ever failed me. You are my soul," I said, feeling like I was in pain. Emotionally, I felt like I was about to break all the way down, but I stood up and laid my head on her chest. "I'm sorry I didn't come right away, momma, but I had bullets in me. I needed to get myself together before I stepped back out. It didn't have nothin' to do with you. You're my angel; you have to know that." I stood up and looked down on her.

She shook her head. "If I would have been doing what I needed to, you would have never had to jump into the dope game. Then, I couldn't even get you the money you needed without damn near getting myself killed. I'm no good for you, baby. You deserve a better mother than me. I'm so stupid with everything." She whimpered and broke down crying.

I felt like I was about to throw up all over the floor. I could not take seeing my mother in that position— knocked down and drug out. She was at her lowest point and I felt like a loser because I didn't know how to bring her out of her darkness.

I kissed her on the swollen lips and laid my head back on to her chest, with my arm wrapped around her protectively. "I love you with everything that I am, momma. Your son is crazy about you, and when you leave this hospital, I'm putting you in your own home with your name on the deed. I'ma buy you a new whip, and help you open a few restaurants like you've always wanted to. I swear from here on out I'm going to be the one taking care of you and keeping you safe. Your baby boy is becoming a man." I kissed her cheeks and stroked her arm.

She smiled weakly. "I love hearing you tell me that you love me, son. It's better than this morphine that they're pumping into my system. All my life, all I've ever wanted was my own little prince, and now that I got you, I just never want to lose your love. You're so perfect to me in every single way. Do you know that?" She asked with tears running down her cheeks.

"I know, momma. You tell me that all the time." I kissed her on the forehead and continued to stroke her arm, doing my best to avoid the IVs that were placed in it.

She sniffled and put her hand on to my back, rubbing it. "That man tried to kill me, Shemar. Had you not come home when you did, he would have. I would be a goner right now. I thank you so much, my baby."

I couldn't do nothing but continue to stroke her arm. I was trying my best to not break down because I was on the verge. No man should ever have to witness their mother in that state. It was making me weaker than I had ever been in my entire life. All of me wanted to leave out of that hospital, find the pastor and blow his brains out, after I tortured his ass nearly to death.

The nurse knocked on the door three times, then opened it. "Sorry, but visiting hours are over. You have less than five minutes to say your goodbyes, then, unfortunately, I'm going to have to ask you leave," said the petite white girl with a million freckles all over her face.

My mother sat up in the bed as best she could, and opened her arms. "Gimme a hug, baby, and tell me how much you love yo' momma. I need to hear it with every fiber of my being," she said in a hoarse voice.

I leaned down and kissed her lips, then wrapped her into my embrace, holding her, and feeling her love radiate all through my body. This was my Queen. The one person that could feed my soul with just a kiss or a hug. A mother to me was like nourishment to the body. I would be weak without her. Lost and broken. For me, she had risked her life, and I would never forget that for as long as I lived. "I love you, momma, and I've missed you so very much, but I'll be back in a few days. Please be strong, because yo' baby boy needs you. I'll always need you; never forget that. Please."

I laid her back and put the sheets over her. Before I left out of the room, I noted that she had a big smile on her face, and that warmed my heart. I would do anything to heal that woman. I mean anything.

I met up with Simone in the lobby. When she saw me, she stood up and came in my direction. "I need to talk to you, Shemar, before you leave. Is that okay?" she asked, looking me over closely.

I nodded. "Yeah, that's cool. Look, Nikki, meet us in the car in like twenty minutes." I put my arm around Simone and walked her out into the parking lot.

As soon as we made it into the car, she took a deep breath and sat back. "So, first of all, how are you doing?"

I could tell that she was up to something. For as long as I knew her, she had never started a conversation off that way. I smiled. "I'm good, Simone. What's on your mind?"

I turned to look at her as an Ambulance rolled up to the hospital with its sirens blaring like crazy. Then, the medics jumped out of the truck and threw open the back door, while about five members of the hospital staff ran out of the hospital to assist them.

Simone looked on curiously just as I did. "Nothin' is really on my mind. I just been missing you of course, and wondering if you'll be at our next doctor's appointment, scheduled for Tuesday. You missed the one for today, but it's my fault for not telling you. I just figured you'd be busy." She looked at the floor of the Bentley, sadly.

I frowned. I didn't like whenever something came up involving her pregnancy and she'd neglect to inform me about it. I wanted to be a part of it every step of the way, no matter what I had going on in my life. I wasn't a deadbeat type nigga. I knew that she had to be a priority, and I made it my business to always be there for her when she called me. I flared my nostrils and tried to calm down. I had to be careful with how I treated Simone because she was very emotional and easily hurt. There was nothing that I hated worse than hurting a female I cared about.

"Baby, please don't be mad at me. I just don't want to crowd you with anything because I know you got so much going on. I don't want that to be the reason you kick me to the curb down the road. I'm just trying to stay in my lane and wait for you to drive down it." She reached over and grabbed my hand.

I tried my best to keep my composure. "Simone, whenever somethin' take place with you or the baby, I want to know about it. I don't want you thinking that you in this thing alone because you're not. I'm gon' do everything that I can to be there for you in every single way. I don't want you needing or wanting for anything, if I can help it. Your only job right now is to birth us a healthy baby." I reached into my pocket and pulled out about five thousand in hundreds and fifties, then handed it to her. "Here. I don't want you to have no less than this in your bank account. I'ma hit you with five gees every week."

She shook her head and pushed the money back to my chest. "Unh, unh, Shemar. I don't want yo' money. You know it ain't never been about that between me and you. That money don't mean shit to me. You do."

I watched them rush the person on the stretcher into the hospital. The Ambulance rolled away and another one pulled up, and the same procedure was repeated. I guess I was looking out of the window because I felt a little offended by her pushing my money back to me. I knew she wasn't a gold digger or nothing like that, and that wasn't what I was getting at. I just didn't like thinking about her not having at least five gees at her disposal at all times. Hood Rich had told me that I was to make sure that the women in my life were taken care of at all times.

Simone was carrying my child. It was my obligation to take care of her to the fullest extent of my abilities. She reached and rubbed my leg. "Shemar, are you mad at me? Did I say something wrong to you just now?"

I didn't give her any eye contact. I was too far gone in my head. I knew that there was something that I was supposed to be saying to Simone to make her feel worthy as a woman, but I was drawing a blank. I wasn't mad at her, but I was pretty sure that my silence was giving her that impression.

I slowly shook my head. "Simone, take this money, baby. I'm not asking you to. I'm telling you. You're the mother of my child. Ain't no way I'm supposed to be walking around with plenty paper and you ain't got none. As long as I know you got at least five bands in yo' pocket every week, then I'll be okay. It'll be more when the baby come. I'ma make sure y'all don't need for absolutely nothin'. I got this," I said, putting the money in her hand and closing her fist around it.

She lowered her head. "You see, that's what I'm afraid of, Shemar. I'm afraid that you're setting things up so that you can take care of me and this baby from a distance. Like you already know that you aren't going to be there as a real father should, and that's what I can't handle. That is what makes me try my best to not reach out to you until I absolutely need you. I don't want to do this alone. I'm so scared. I need you with me every step of the way. I'm just a little girl." She dropped the money in her lap and put both of her hands over her face, crying into them. "I swear to God, I love you so freaking much. I think about you all day long. I'm always so worried about you and wonder if you're thinking of me. I don't want to just be a baby momma. I am not a statistic. You can't allow for me to be." She broke down harder.

I tilted back my head with my face towards the ceiling. Damn. What the fuck was I gon' do? I was being pulled in so many different directions, so many people's emotions were tied into me and I didn't want to be the cause of hurting any one of them. Each woman had a different purpose in my life. I loved them in their own way. On the flip side, I felt like they all loved and needed me for different reasons, and it was my job to step up to the plate on all levels. In this moment, Simone was most important because she was growing our child inside of her body. Not only that, but she had gone out on the limb, giving me her virginity when we were just seventeen years old.

I had to hold her down. I had to be her knight under all circumstances. I didn't know how I was going to figure everything out, but I also didn't have a choice. I had to step all the way up all around the board.

I wrapped my arm around her shoulder and pulled her to me, kissing her sexy lips, before sliding my tongue in her mouth, wrestling with her own. She sucked all over my lips, and tongued me back; getting closer to me, breathing all hard. She was turning me on to say the least, but I knew we couldn't take it there, so I needed to calm down. I broke the kiss and sat back in my seat with my heart pounding in my chest.

Simone wasn't trying to hear that shit. She straddled me slowly, then leaned down and kissed my lips again. Her baby bump was against my chest. Her skirt was around her waist, exposing her bikini underwear designed by Prada. "I want some of you, baby. I just wanna feel you inside of my body right now. Maybe that will help me calm down some because I'm so fucking emotional." She sucked on my lips and started to unbuckle my belt.

"Wait, Simone, we can't do this shit right here. You see all them ambulances and stuff running in and out of here. That'll be crazy," I said, feeling her bite into my neck, causing my dick to get super hard.

She sat up and groaned. "Then park somewhere else, but you finna give me some of my dick. I ain't taking no for an answer." She reached between us and slid her hand into my pants, squeezing my dick, and biting into my neck again.

I lost all the will power I had inside of me at that point. As soon as I started the ignition so I could drive away and find somewhere else to park, Nikki came walking out of the hospital, before I could drive away from our parking spot. She jogged to the car, opened the back door and got in. Simone jerked her head up and looked into the backseat at her.

"Damn, Shemar. What? Y'all was finna leave me or somethin'?" she asked angrily.

Simone cut in. "N'all, we wasn't finna do that, but he gon' park somewhere that's ducked off, so I can get some of his pipe. If you wait inside, I'll have him text you when we done."

I was curious to see what Nikki was gon' say, though I had already thrown the car in drive. I was hoping they didn't get into an argument because Simone had me riled all the way up. I needed to hit that pussy for about ten minutes, then I'd be good. At least that's how I was thinking.

Nikki sucked her teeth. "Hell n'all. It's plenty police going in and out of that hospital. Y'all can do whatever y'all finna do with me right back here. I done seen him fuck before. It ain't no big deal. Shemar, you betta tell her."

I didn't even care by this point. I was rubbing all over Simone's ass with one hand and steering with the other. I drove out of the parking lot and down the street a lil' bit, pulling up in the parking lot of a closed bakery. Soon as the car was off, I pulled Simone's panties to the side and slid that hot pussy down my dick while she dug her nails into my shoulder blades.

"Ummm-Shemar." She rose all the way up, then back down again, riding me in a steady motion. That shit was feeling extra good. "Umm. Umm. Umm. Umm. Umm. Shemar. Umm. Umm. Yes, baby. Uhh! Yes." She bounced up and down on me while I held her big ass. It felt soft in my hands. That pregnant pussy oozed all over my dick, making it that much better.

I smacked her on it. "Come on, baby, get yours before we torture Nikki back there. Ride me fast, lil' momma." I smacked her ass again.

"Ah! Shit! Okay. Okay. Okay. Umm. Yes. Yes. Here. I. Go. Yes. Shemar. Shemar. Shemar. Umm. Umm. Uhhhh! Shit, yes! Umm. Umm. Umm. Umm." She moaned, riding me at full speed now while the car rocked back and forth.

I pulled her shoulder straps down and exposed her brown titties, sucking all over, them, trapping the nipples with my lips, and pulling on 'em. Her pussy slid up and down my pipe in a squishy fashion—nice and hot, oozing its delight and sending me on a journey at the same time. Simone moaned in my ear, but then I could also hear the faint moans of Nikki coming from the backseat. I tried to turn around to see what she was doing, but Simone wouldn't let me.

She leaned all the way over and continued to ride me faster and faster. "Uhhhh! Shemar!" She moved to the side and I saw Nikki's hand come up and grab her titty, pulling on her nipple, then groping her breast. The sight of her touching her really drove me crazy.

"Fuck that pregnant pussy, Shemar. Hit that shit! Ummm! Y'all making me go nuts back here. Unnnn! Shit. Here I cum. Uhhhhh!" She hollered with her hand leaving Simone's breasts and trailing down to my chest, squeezing it. Then she leaned over the seat and sucked on the side of my neck while she continued to moan. That threw me for a loop because for as long as me and Nikki had been friends we had never gotten down together on that level.

I mean, I know she'd just opened up to me, but I was still unsure as to how I really felt about us crossing the line, although sexually she drove me crazy.

Simone sped up the pace and got to riding me so fast and hard that I couldn't help getting ready to cum deep within that pregnant pussy. She tilted her head back and let out a piercing scream before cumming all over me. "Ahhhhhhhhh! Dadddddeeeee- a!"

Her pussy's walls started to vibrate, and that pushed me over the edge. I came deep within her womb with my eyes closed.

Afterwards, we pulled back up to the main entrance of the hospital and Simone asked me if I'd get out and holler at her for a second, so I did.

She walked into my face and stood on her tippy toes, kissing my lips. "Thank you, Shemar, because I really needed that. Like I said before, I ain't trying to cramp yo' style or tie you down just yet. I know we're still young and got a lot of growing up to do. Just don't forget about me from time to time, and when you are ready to settle down, let me be that one that you settle down with. Okay?" Before I could say anything, she wrapped her arms around my neck. "You ain't gotta make no decisions just yet, but never forget what I said. Oh, and thank for the money. I'll make it last for a lil' while."

I held her in my arms. "You ain't gotta do that. I already told you that I'ma hit you with that at least once a week just because I appreciate you. And when it's time to do the whole family one on one thing, I can definitely see you as being my wife. I mean that." I kissed her lips again, and rubbed her back, before taking a step back and looking into her pretty face. Then, I placed my hand on her stomach. "Every appointment, I'll be there, every time. You hear me?"

She smiled and nodded. "I hear you."

Nikki rolled down her window then stuck her head out of it. "Shemar, bring yo' ass on. You know we ain't supposed to be on these white folks' streets this late at night. You gon' get our ass hung. Kiss her and let her walk off."

Simone scrunched her face, then took a deep breath, looking up at me. "Well, I love you, baby, and I hope to see you soon. Hit me up on Facebook later once you settle in. You know, just so I can know you made it back to wherever you are safely."

I kissed her one more time and gripped that ass. "I will, baby. Tell momma that I love her, and you be safe. Protect our child."

Ghost

Chapter 6

The next morning, Purity woke me up with breakfast in bed. I opened my eyes to her kissing my lips. "Wake up, Shemar, so I can put somethin' on yo' stomach, because I know you ain't ate nothin' all night." She rubbed my chest, then reached over and grabbed the tray of food.

I sat up in the bed and yawned, stretching my arms way over my head. I was exhausted. After doing the most with Simone, and then getting back to the mansion at damn near four in the morning, I felt like I'd just went to sleep. I blinked a few times then turned to look at her before smiling, because she was already done up with makeup on and everything. She looked like she was prepared for a night out on the town or something.

"Damn, Purity, why you all made up and shit? Where you think you finna go?" I asked, sitting the tray of food on my lap, while she cut a piece off of the sausage with a knife, and fed it to me on a fork.

"Well, if you must know, me and Jahliya are going shopping. She told me not to bring nothing but my pretty face, so that's what I'm doing. But before I left out with her, I wanted to make sure that you had something on your stomach. So, eat up," she demanded.

I chewed the sausage and swallowed it, before she cut into the cheesy omelet and put it into my mouth as well. "You ain't ask me if you can go nowhere," I said with a mouthful of food. I was hoping that we weren't about to argue because I didn't want to go there with her, but I didn't like her just jumping up and thinking she was about to do something that she had not gotten my permission to do. I mean, she was still my little sister and I guess I was kind of overprotective of her.

She smirked. "First of all, stop talking with your mouthful because that's rude. I'm pretty sure Vicki and her family taught you better than that." She held the glass of orange juice to my lips and I took a sip out of it.

"Purity, stop playin' with me."

"Secondly, we're going shopping, and her mother will be there. It's not like I'm doing too much. I need some new clothes, and she say she gon' fit the bill, so why not? She already told me she ain't talking about no cheap stuff, so I'm all in. You literally gon' have to whoop my ass to keep me from going to get a bunch of new clothes and shoes, and you wouldn't do that to yo' baby girl, now would you?" she asked, sticking her bottom lip out like a child.

I couldn't do nothing but laugh at that. "N'all, I could never put my hands on you and you know it. But from now on, just holler at me ahead of time so I know what's going on. It ain't sweet with this family. Taurus is worse than me. That fool got all kinds of enemies that wouldn't hesitate to hurt his people, females and all. You gotta be careful, do you understand me?"

She fed me another bite of omelet, then wiped my mouth with a napkin. "I hear you loud and clear, but the only thing I'm thinking is that if you don't want me going with them, then why don't you take me shopping and blow a bag on me? What you can't make time to do that or something?" she asked, raising her left eye brow.

Before I could answer her, there was a knock on the door. "Who is it?" I yelled, feeling somewhat annoyed because I felt like Purity was trying to say something without actually saying it. I didn't like when she held her true feelings and thoughts inside. I felt like we could tell each other exactly what was on our minds because we had that kind of bond. It was special, and I didn't want to lose that.

"It's Jahliya. I just wanna know if Purity is ready to roll out. The limo is ready, and my mother is already inside of it, looking impatient."

Purity leaned forward and kissed me on the lips. "Gotta go, Shemar, but I promise I'll be careful, and don't be mad at me. I really do listen to you, and I appreciate how much you care about me. It makes me feel loved."

I watched her grab her Gucci purse and make her way out of the room. Before she opened the door, she blew me a kiss, then disappeared. I ate a little more of the food, drank the juice and passed back out from exhaustion.

The next time I woke up, Nikki was pushing me on the chest. "Shemar, you gotta get up and go shower. Taurus say you gotta holler at Vito tonight in San Antonio. Y'all gon' roll out in an hour."

Once again, I yawned and got up, getting myself ready while Nikki sat on the bed and watched me like I was a movie or something.

"Nikki, what's good with that fool Nut? Why I ain't seen him in a few days?" I asked, turning on the shower in the bathroom, then walking back into the bedroom where she was rolling a blunt.

"I forgot to tell you that my cousin had to run back to New York because one of his homies got killed out there. He left three days ago. He supposed to be handling something for Hood Rich while he out there. He said he'll be back in a week or so. I thought I told you that," she said, licking up and down the blunt, then put fire to it.

I shook my head. "N'all, you ain't tell me that, because if you would have, I would have never asked you about it." I exhaled, stepped into the bathroom and into the stall, feeling the hot beads of water crash into my skin right away. I grabbed a towel and loaded it up with body wash, and got to handling my business.

My mind was on my next mission. Taurus wanted Vito dead, and I was all for that. Once I put Vito in the dirt, then I could focus on building my own empire. I wanted it all. I wanted to make sure that the ladies of my life never had to want or need for anything. Behind the lids of my eyes were a dynasty. A dynasty that I would construct from the ground up. I smiled as the water crashed into my face, then I heard the stall open.

My eyes shot open as I saw Nikki climb into the stall with her back facing my chest. The water poured down on her hair, turning it curly right away. She backed into me until her ass was against my front. I bit into my bottom lip at the soft feel of it, wrapping my arm around her stomach and pulling her back to me.

"Ummm. I just figured since you were showering that I would get clean, too. We ain't trying to run they water bill up or nothin', am I right?" She laughed, moving her ass up and down my dick.

I trailed my hand around until it was on her bald pussy lips, running my fingers over them, and sliding one inside of her box. Her cat was meaty. Way fatter than I could have ever imagined, and tight. It seemed to lock around the one finger that I had buried within her.

I leaned forward and bit into her neck. "Nikki, why you playin' with me right now? You already know what I'd do to this pussy. I'm trying to keep my cool and not take it there with you, but you making it so hard." I meant that literally. My dick was stuck all the way up and poking her in the ass. In fact, the head was actually between her ass cheeks, laying up against the rose bud back there. I took a step forward, impaling him further between them.

"Ummm. Shemar, you been looking at my ass ever since we were lil' kids. I bet you'd fuck it if I let you, huh?" She backed into me and moved her ass from side to side while I played in her pussy and sucked on her neck. "Ummm. You making me wet."

I slid a second finger into her, and tried to inch my dick further into her ass cheeks. Her heat was amazing and was doing something to me that I can't explain. "Give me this ass, Nikki. You know I wanna hit yo' strapped ass. Ever since we were little, that ass always been fat. Let me see what it do." I groaned, feeling my dick throbbed against her.

She leaned all the way forward, grabbed the bottle of body wash, and handed it to me. "Hurry up,

Shemar, before I change my mind. Fuck my ass since you want it so bad, but just hurry up because I need it right now. Mmmm-a!"

I started fingering her pussy faster while she spread her legs and leaned forward like I was about to search her or something. Her fat pussy jumped out from the back and I had second thoughts on wanting to hit that ass. I wanted some of that kitty. I could just tell that she had a shot on her, and I wanted to see what that was like.

She smacked herself on the ass hard. Her cheeks jiggled and shook along with her thighs. "Hurry up, Shemar. Give me some of that pipe!"

I stepped forward and ran my dick up and down her pussy lips, preparing to slide into her when she reached back and moved my dick. I frowned, then tried to put him at her pussy again. But she stopped me. "Nikki, what's good?" I asked, getting frustrated. By this point, I wanted some of her pussy so bad that I was hurting.

It was early in the morning and I had just woke up. One thing about a healthy man is that when he first wakes up, that's when he is at his horniest. She'd seduced me enough. Her body was banging and now that I had seen how she felt on the inside, I wanted a real tour. I was feening.

She stood up and turned around, looking into my eyes while the water beat against her titties. Her areolas covered most of her breast. Both nipples stood out a cool inch, and even the sight of them were driving me mad. She slid her hand between her legs and squeezed her sex lips, then slid a middle finger inside herself. Then, she dropped down to her knees, reached up and took my dick into her hand, stroking it while the water splashed into her gorgeous face.

I took her hand off of my dick and pulled her up. "I don't want no head, Nikki. I'm good on that," I said, cuffing her pretty titties, sucking first one nipple and then the next.

"Ummm. Shemar, you just too much." She moaned and started to finger herself at full speed. "Keep touching me, please. Just let me get this one off. I'll get you back, I promise." She opened her legs wider and really went to town.

I frowned, sucked on her titties for a little while longer, then picked her ass up, making her wrap her legs around me, carrying her into the bathroom and laying her on the floor. Afterward, I crawled between her legs, pushing her knees to her chest and sucking her sex lips into my mouth while she played with her clitoris. I slurped loudly, and got to fingering her as fast as my wrist would go.

"Huh! Huh! Huh-a! Ooooo-a! Oooo-a! Yes! Ooo-a! Ooooo! Oooo-a! Uhhh! I'm cumming! Oooooo-a!" She humped into my face again and again, then started to cum all over her thighs.

I continued to suck on her sex lips, then trapped her clit and sucked it like a berry while her pretty feet went onto my shoulders, kicking wildly. After she came, I laid on top of her and tongued her down while I ran my dick head up and down her slit. Her juices poured out of her like a tub that was over flowing. I wanted to fuck her so bad, but every time I tried to put him inside, she would stop me.

I started to wonder if something was wrong. "Nikki, what's good?"

She held my hand and tried to sit up, but I had her little ass in a ball. I had plans on killing that pussy with all of my might. I had watched that ass go from being somewhat flat when we were kids, to coming out when we became young teenagers. I felt like I wanted to enjoy her entire body. My dick was aching.

"Shemar, I ain't never fucked no nigga before. I know you think I have, but I really haven't. I'm scared that if you fuck me, I'm gon' be psychotic over yo' ass, and you already got enough of that going around. We supposed to be homies. I don't wanna break that bond." She bit into her bottom lip and looked so sexy. It was killing me. That and how my dick felt laid up against her hot pussy. She inadvertently opened her legs, and my piece slipped between her lips, now lying on her hole to the Promise Land.

"Nikki, I'm begging you, let me hit this shit. I don't care if you get crazy. I want some of this pussy. I been feening for you for a long time. You said you got needs, so let me meet them. I won't fail you." I was ready to break down. I wanted to hit that cat so bad.

She took her legs off of my shoulders and opened them wide. Then, she took her fingers and opened her lips. "Shemar, just as bad as you want me, I need you. I'm just scared. I don't want to mess up what we have. I know I'm a real jealous person. It ain't gon' be just fucking to me. Its gon' be a whole lot more than that, and I ain't gon' be able to help it. Please, listen to me when I tell you this, because I'm crazy, Shemar. I'm already feeling some type of way about you and you ain't went in me yet. That's gon' make it way worst."

I took my dick and slowly guided him past her lips. I heard everything she was saying, but I wanted that body. I had to be inside of it. The further my dick went in, the more excited I got.

She tried to back away and get up off of the floor, but I pulled her back down and got between her legs more firmly. They wrapped around me and squeezed me tight. "I'm not giving you none of this pussy, Shemar. If you want this shit bad enough, you gon' have to take it." Once again, she tried to wiggle away, but I pulled her back to me and forced her thighs further apart.

I clenched my jaw. "So, this how you gon' do me Nikki? Huh? You gon' make me take this shit?" I asked, laying all of my weight on her. I took my dick and put it back at her entrance, slowly forcing the head inside.

"Unnn! Fuck you! Get off of me, Shemar!" She sounded out of breath. Though she was telling me to get off of her, she made no more attempts to scoot back or push me away. "Please. Don't do this."
I was too far gone, feening for her box. I had to have it. I had to know what she felt like. I slammed forward and impaled her on my dick, pulled back and slammed it home again, before I got to beating it up.

"Uhhhh! Nooo! Uh! Uh! Uh! Uh! Uh! Uh! Mmm-a! Mmm-a! Shemar! You fuckin' me! You fuckin meeeee-a!" She reached up and pulled me down so that I was on top of her.

She licked my lips, then sucked them into her mouth as my dick crashed into her with force, over and over again. Our skins slapped together. The steam in the bathroom mixed with the scents of our sexing bodies. The aroma added to my bliss. Her pussy felt like a tight, wet latex glove that milked me. I'd crossed the line with Nikki, and in that moment, it wasn't registering. The only thing that mattered was the space in between our legs, and it felt so good.

"No! No! No! Shemar! I'm gon' love. I'm gon' love you too much! This. This. Uhhh-a! This shit! Ummm-a! This shouldn't have happened!" She wrapped her legs around me tighter and hugged me, sucking all over my neck while my dick pistoled into her center, harder and harder. When her nails went into my back and scratched until they drew blood, I didn't pay it no mind. Then, she blinked tears, and moaned with her mouth wide open. "Huh! Uh! Uh! Uh! I'm cumming! I'm cumming again. Uhhh-fuck it feel so good-a! Cum in me, Shemar! Cum in me, baby!"

My hips got to going so fast that I had to hold her tighter. Now I was biting on her neck like a vampire, putting my gangsta down on that pussy before I came deep within her.

After we showered, we stood in front of the mirror, getting ourselves together. I watched her brush her long, curly hair into a pony tail while I oiled my stomach and chest. We made eye contact through our reflections.

She stopped brushing her hair and turned to me. "I hope you was listening to what I told you back there, Shemar. I'm finna try my best to go insane over you, but I already know what's finna happen.

You betta be able to handle it since you took my pussy and all." She smiled at saying the last part.

I sucked my teeth. "So, you really gone run with that shit, huh? You gone sit yo' pretty ass here and make it seem like I took the pussy? Really?"

She bugged her eyes and shrugged, holding her shoulders up as if she were innocent. "What? You did. I was trying to have a nice shower, but you had to go ahead and take what you wanted. If I recall, I told you no more than once, and no is supposed to mean no, but I see how that worked out for me." She laughed and started to brush her hair again.

I looked at her for a long time. I felt myself getting a lil' irritated at what she was implying, but then I cast it aside because I knew the truth. I felt like she was looking ahead, and if things ever blew up between us, then she could say that it was my fault for crossing the line. She wouldn't have to share the blame, and that was cool because I intended on holding her down even more so now.

I stepped behind her and sucked on her neck while I ran my hands up and down her flat stomach, moving them upward and cupping her tits.

"Ummm-a. There you go again, Shemar, just taking possession of my body. You don't own me." She sucked on her bottom lip and made eye contact with me in the mirror.

I kissed her neck softly. "You and I know what it is, and no matter what just happened, I love you and I been loving you ever since we were kids. You still my right-hand man, and I still need you to have my back. I don't trust nobody in them slums but you. You my rider and my baby. Never forget yo' place."

She nodded, looking me in the eyes. "I won't, and thank you, Shemar. Now, hold me down like you supposed to."

There was no doubt about it, I would.

Chapter 7

Later that night, me and Taurus staked out across from the room that Vito was supposed to be laid up in with one of the strippers from Taurus' club. I had a black ski mask on my lap, and a fat ass blunt in my hand that Taurus had rolled. He said it was stuffed with Tropical Loud, straight from Oahu, Hawaii.

I didn't know if it really was or not, but after a few pulls, I felt like I was on an island all by myself. I was mellow, and the thought of killing Vito didn't affect me one bit. I also had a few Oxy's in my system because my shoulder was fuckin with me a lil' bit.

Taurus wiped the blade of his knife on a black rag. He looked like he was angry. "You know, Shemar, I knew from day one that I didn't like this nigga Vito when one of my lil' broads introduced me to him back in the day. But back then, I needed this nigga so I could move out of Memphis. I had a lot of heat on me at that time, and Vito and Flyy were my exit out of my city, and into theirs." He shook his head. "I came down here and Hood Rich put me in the game with the Rebirth. That fuck nigga Vito started getting over on me right away and didn't think I knew it." He held the blade up to the light and checked it over before handing it to me.

I took it and put it back into my holster that he had given me. "So, why you ain't body him back then and get it over with?"

I was curious to know that because it would give me a little insight as to how Taurus got down when he put somebody in the game. If he was the type that killed you right away, that meant there was very little room for error when it came to operating under him. On the other hand, if he waited, then it just meant that he liked to play with his food before he killed it, and that he was always aware, even when you thought he wasn't. That was scarier to me because it meant I had to always try and out think him, or simply stay on the straight and narrow. That was hard to do in the game, because you couldn't ever say how one day was going to go over the next.

Taurus took another blade off of the bed and started to wipe it down. I didn't know why he wanted to shine them up first when all we were going to do was cover them in Vito's blood, but I didn't question him about it. "I got a lot of love for Vito's cousin Blaze. Had it not been for her, I would have wasted him way back when." He looked at me head on. "I don't play about my money, Shemar. I will murder a nigga's whole family tree over my scratch. Second to my money is loyalty. If a nigga says that he is giving me his loyalty and he goes back and breaks it, I could never walk this green earth without feeling betrayed to my very core. Money and loyalty is everything to me, and once you reach that kingpin status it will become the same to you. This game is cold as ice, so you must rule this bitch with an iron fist. Everything I got is because of my loyalty to Hood Rich. I am to him what I expect you to be to me, lil' homie. I see a whole lot of me in you. That's why I gotta get you to where you need to be." His phone buzzed, causing him to stand up and look down at it, before nodding. "Hell yeah, let's go. That nigga in the shower right now, and shorty on her way out the room."

I slid my mask down my face and picked up my pistol, placing it in the small of my back. Ten minutes later, there was a knock on our door. Taurus opened it and Eve stepped into the room, looking like a fucking Goddess. Her long hair dropped to her waist, and she had her body stuffed inside of a Dolce and Gabbana cat suit that complimented her frame. She stepped into the room with the matching red bottoms on her feet, walked up to Taurus and kissed him on the lips with her eyes closed.

"Hey, daddy. I did everything, just like you told me to. He in the shower right now, and should be out in ten minutes. I didn't like letting him touch me, but I'll do anything for you, daddy. I gotta go and wash my body because I feel sick on the stomach." She made a face like she was getting ready to hurl.

Taurus wrapped her into his arms, rubbing the sides of her face. "Look at me, Eve. Why did I name you Eve? Tell me?"

She blinked and looked him in the eyes. "You said you named me Eve because I am your tempter. I am the one that get these niggas to bite that apple before they are kicked out of the garden of your dynasty. You said you chose me because I am the most alluring Queen in your stable."

He leaned forward and kissed her lips again. "I'll meet you back in Dallas. Tell Princess that you're sleeping with us tonight because you earned it. Go, baby."

I had to admit that I liked how that nigga Taurus got down. He had a swag that I wanted to adopt into the fiber of my being.

Three minutes later, we were creeping into Vito's room after sliding the keycard in and out of the lock. As soon as we stepped into it, I could still hear the shower water going on full blast. This nigga had the nerve to be singing a Sam Smith song at the top of his lungs. That shit made me snicker before that killa came back into my soul. I wanted to torture this nigga and I was going to enjoy it.

I stepped into the bathroom and opened the shower door, before slapping him in the face with my pistol just enough to make him open his eyes and shut up. He was fucking dude song up and it was annoying as hell. He flew back into the wall and threw his hands up, opening his eyes wide, looking like a deer caught in headlights. I wanted to take my mask off right there so bad just to really give his ass a scare, but it wasn't the time for me to be playing games. I had Taurus watching me real close, and Vito's murder was my key to the streets.

"Hey, man, I ain't got more than ten gees in my pocket. You can have that shit, my nigga. It ain't worth dying over," he said, sounding like a bitch to me.

I grabbed him by his neck and pulled his naked ass out of the shower with my pistol against his temple, slinging him to the floor and throwing his boxers from the bathroom counter at him. "Nigga, shut yo' bitch ass up and put them boxers on. I don't wanna see yo' naked ass body. Hurry up!"

He crawled on the floor, grabbed the boxers and slid them on before putting his hands back into the air. "Say, Potna, you let me skate on this lick, mane, and I'll put fifty gees in yo' pocket. Now, I know you ain't hitting licks that's grossing that. Fuck with me in this one, my nigga." He lowered his eyes and looked me over closely for any signs of me considering his offer.

I cocked the hammer on my pistol, then grabbed him up by his dreads, and threw him out of the bathroom into the bedroom where Taurus was waiting for him. "Have a seat, Vito, and don't make no muthafuckin' noise or it's curtains for you, my nigga. I know you recognize my voice, so you know this ain't a game right now. Sit yo' punk ass down."

Vito stood up and sat into the chair that Taurus had placed next to the fire place.

"Damn, Taurus, man. What all this about? I ain't did nothing for you to be visiting me under these circumstances."

I walked across the white carpet and put my pistol to the side of his neck while Taurus tied his wrists to the chair, then his ankles together. I could tell that Vito wanted to resist but knew that it wouldn't have been in his best interest.

After he was bound to the chair, Taurus put his pistol back in its holster, and I put mine in the small of my back. I was a street nigga and wasn't used to having holsters and shit. I felt most comfortable when my pistol was ducked off back there.

Taurus walked up to him, and kneeled in front of him, looking him in the face. "I made sure you and yo' family ate from the moment I stepped foot in Houston. I didn't know you from Adam, Vito, and before I could even get my feet wet in the game out here, you and that nigga Flyy was scheming off the top like I didn't know it or somethin'. But on the strength of Blaze, I looked the other way and let you keep yo' life." He lowered his head and shook it. "One thing I don't like about you Houston boys is that you don't know how to stop digging a bigger hole once you get into one, and the shovel you been using this far is caked in mud."

Vito struggled against his binds and looked from me to Taurus with his eyes bucked. "Taurus, I don't know what you getting at, but I ain't have shit to do with Emilio getting at yo' men. I swear I didn't set that up. That came from another way. You gotta believe me," he said, trying to unloosen his wrist with no success.

Taurus smiled and looked up at me shaking his head. "You see this shit? Now I ain't said nothing about the Emilio hit; this fool just offered it. That's what I mean by digging big holes. Nigga, you done did so much wrong that you don't know why I'm on yo' ass right now." He frowned and stood up. "Who arranged my hit then, nigga, if you didn't? Tell me, because some real special people that's close to me caught some slugs that wasn't meant for them, and one was a female." He reached and smacked him so hard that he spilt the side of his nose. A trickle of blood leaked down on to his collarbone.

Vito yelped and almost fell out of the chair. His titties shook on his chest. He looked back up to Taurus with fear in his eyes. "The Zoe's man. Them niggas trying to bomb at you all the way from Miami. They got Emilio 'nem involved by putting five hundred thousand on yo' head, and a promise that they would do business with the Mexican Cartel once they settled in this way. Some big wig by the name of Yohan." Vito looked from Taurus to me in fear. "I swear I'm not lying to you, Taurus. I put that on my daughter, man."

Taurus lowered his eyes into slits under his mask, then reached and grabbed Vito by his thick neck. "Bitch nigga, you promised me yo' loyalty. You gave me yo' shit and promised it in blood, so why in the fuck didn't you let me know when all of this shit went down, huh? How could you arrange for the meeting, and help them set me up? What the fuck kind of loyalty is that?"

Vito swallowed and struggled against his binds once again. "I ain't no snitch, Taurus. You know I don't get down like that. If it's one thing you can count on with me it's that my lips ain't ever loose like that."

Taurus looked at him for a long time, then looked back to me. "You hear this dumb ass nigga? His lips ain't ever loose like that. Ain't that a bitch." He took a step back and grabbed the duct tape off of the bed. "Well, we ain't ever gotta worry about yo' lips being loose again, now do we?" He took a long strip and bit it off of the roll.

"Taurus, please. Don't do this. Don't, ummm, ummm, ummm." He hollered as Taurus taped his mouth shut.

"Lil homie, this nigga is yo' key to the streets. Now, I wanna sit right there and enjoy you kill this nigga. Buss into this game with a vengeance. Make this nigga pay for his sins in honor of me. Put yo' loyalty in blood."

Vito struggled against his binds and shook his head. His eyes looked like they wanted to jump out of his head, and I felt nothing, but anger on how he did the homie Taurus. Anger and excitement.

I nodded and slipped the Kitana blade out of its holster, and stepped up to Vito. "How you want it?" I asked, looking over my shoulder at Taurus.

"Ummm! Ummm! Ummm!" Vito was going crazy now, rocking his chair from side to side in a mock attempt to get away. He shook his head and hollered into the duct tape.

Taurus sat on the bed. "Just make him pay. This is yo' key, lil' homie."

I nodded again, stepped forward, grabbed Vito by the neck, and sliced him across the face with the blade, once, twice, then four times in a row, finally looking over my shoulder at Taurus for approval.

He nodded and stood up. "This bitch nigga gave his loyalty in blood, so his blood is what he must pay for dishonoring it. Fuck this nigga over, lil' homie. Buss into the game. He is yo' key!"

"Ummm! Ummm!" Vito whimpered in pain.

I took the knife, pushed his forehead back, and stabbed him ten times in the neck, before cutting his throat, over killing his bitch ass. Since he was gon' be my key to the streets, I had to make a statement to Taurus to let him know that I was not playing when it came to all of this shit. I ain't like Vito anyway, because the first time I met him, he tried to treat me by upping a pistol on me in front of Nikki, so there was bad blood there from the start.

I took a step back and looked over my work. Vito laid with his head in his lap, with blood pouring out of him at a rapid pace.

Taurus walked over to him and pulled him up by the hair, looking into his face, before shaking his head. "I tried my best to not end this nigga on the strength of Blaze, but it's only so much a muhfucka can let slide." He let his head go and it dropped back into his lap. "Let's get the fuck up out of here, lil' homie. Mission accomplished."

Ghost

Chapter 8

It took a full month before I was actually given my buildings in Cloverland. I didn't know why it was taking so long, but trust me when I tell you that every single day it was all I had on my brain. I was ready to get started and ready to get my money right. So, while it took Taurus a full month before he allowed me to step into the game, as soon as the day came, it hit me hard.

He woke me up at five in the morning on a Thursday and we jumped into his Range Rover. "Aiight, Shemar, now you gotta be ready to go because it's time to get money like you supposed to. I'm gon' introduce you to some lil' niggas that's gon' be workin' under you. These my lil' hittas, and they cut from my fabric, so you ain't gotta worry about none of that flakey shit. You got eight buildings over here on Peyton Place, right in the heart of Junkie Alley. Most of the people over here already addicted to the Rebirth, but it's some new heads that just moved in. That's for you to get them addicted to our product. Now, what you gotta remember is that this Rebirth is some strong shit. It's chemically cut so that whoever try this shit, they'll never be able to turn away from it. It's gon' be times when yo' dope fiends gon' come to you with damn near ten gees, and others when they ain't gon' have a pot to piss in. Now, on those times, they'll never forget how you treat them. These hypes will kill you over this dope, Shemar, so never let yo' status allow for you to get too far away from humility. You must put a system in place so that it always works out for you and them.

The goal is to make as much money as possible, while keeping your enemy levels low. You can't really make money and war at the same time, and the last thing you need to be doing is warring with yo' customers." He pulled on to the highway and got to coasting with Money Bag Yo banging out of the speakers. "Any questions, lil' homie?"

I nodded. "What would yo' first move be? You know, like on the first day?" I looked him over closely and leaned more toward him so I could hear what he was about to say over the music. I fucked with Money Bag Yo, but right then wasn't the time for me to be focusing on his music. That nigga was already rich I assumed, and I was trying to get there.

"Well, first thing first: When we get here, the lil' homies should be just about done bagging up them two kilos we gave them last night, so you go in there and assess your profits to come, while at the same time letting these lil' niggas know who you is. It's all about an understanding, as long as the niggas that work under you and respect you, they'll be loyal to you for a long time. At least, that's how it's supposed to go. The game ain't perfect, and for the most part its unpredictable, which is why you must read every man in your outfit and learn their strengths and weaknesses without them even knowing you know them. Once you learn them, then you must find a way to make sure that both their strength and their weaknesses can benefit you and your operation in one way or the other. The first key to the game is capitalization. You must capitalize off of everything and everybody. It's important for advancement." He turned up the sounds and started to nod his head.

"Don't worry, I ain't gone leave yo' side for a few weeks until we get everything down pact. You my protege. I vouched for you which means that every step you make, whether right or wrong, falls on me."

My head was spinning like crazy. Taurus had so much game that went over my head that I was hoping he stayed close until I could soak most of it up. He was a successful Drug Lord in my eyes and what I aspired to be. he was the first man that I looked up to and it felt good having a role model that fit into what I wanted to be in the future. You see, I wasn't one of those lil' boys that wanted to be an NBA basketball player, or a football player. N'all, I wanted to be a hustler. I wanted to take over my slums and build them up the way I wanted them to be. I had visions in my head for my city, and it wasn't all circled around negativity. I honestly wanted to get my paper up so I could empower my people by opening Boys and Girls Clubs for the youth, and making sure that the single mothers in my ghetto didn't have to struggle as much. I wanted to put something in place to ensure that they'd have everything that they needed. I didn't know exactly what that was as of yet, but I knew that I would figure it out down the line.

We got to the buildings about twenty minutes later. When we pulled up in front of the row houses, about five niggas ran from the side of the buildings with pistols in their hands and half-masks covering their faces.

I saw it right away, and upped my .40 caliber, pulling Taurus down to the floor of the truck. "It's a hit, Taurus, get down!" I hollered as I saw the niggas coming up on his side of the truck. I cocked my pistol and aimed for the first dude's head, getting ready to pull the trigger when Taurus slapped my hand away, shocking the shit out of me.

"Wait, Shemar! Them my hittas!" he hollered.

I was literally a second away from pulling the trigger. I looked back over at the niggas and saw that they were posted outside of Taurus's door as if on security.

He sat up and rolled down the window. "What good, Risky? I see you on point," Taurus said, looking behind him at his crew of armed men.

Risky was a heavy-set dude, dark skinned with the eyes of a wolf. He must've had in some white contact lenses. They made him look crazy as hell. "I pledge allegiance to you, Taurus, plus the security detail is my thing. Even though that nigga Flyy ain't in power no more, that don't mean that I don't handle my business. I ain't trying to get replaced. I'm eating too good, fuckin' with you, man." He smiled and I peeped he had a mouth full of gold. "Who dat iz over dere?" he asked, nodding in my direction.

Taurus curled his lip. "This the new boss. His name Shemar, and he my lil' brother. Muhfucka see him and betta respect him, just like they do me, because I'm turning all this over to him. That lil' section that Vito held down, too. He was raised in Cloverland, and he gon' make sure you niggas keep eating."

Risky looked into my eyes and nodded in a *whut up* fashion. "What it do, man? You gon' keep shit the same or you gon' change it up a bit? I know Taurus can vouch for my gunplay. I'll keep you safe out here, homeboy, just like the homie."

I grunted. "I'm just observing for now, but if the homie saying you one hundred, then you ain't got shit to worry about. I ain't trying to switch up too much shit. It's all about loyalty and eating for me. Cloverland is my home, and sooner or later I wanna build it up the way it's supposed to be. It's too many of our people out here starving, especially these mothers. All this paper that we gon' get needs to be reinvested into our community, so our women ain't gotta depend on this racist ass government so much."

Both Taurus and Risky looked at me with eyes wide open as if they couldn't believe what I was saying. I don't know what was making me feel that way, but I was, and I was trying to put things together in my head already.

Risky lead us into the first building with five of his men surrounding us, with their hands under their shirts. The sun was beaming hard, and the humidity was killing me. It felt like it was two hundred degrees outside. The vest on my chest was itching underneath already, and I felt sweat pouring down my back, and I really didn't sweat easily.

When we stepped into the first house, as soon as the door opened, I looked in and saw two dudes with assault rifles on each side of it, with evil scowls on their faces. They saw Taurus and looked up to him without taking the mugs from their faces.

Taurus put his arm around my shoulder as we stepped in. "You see, Shemar, this how you gotta have niggas. Now, watch how I control these killas with just a few hundred. Peep this shit."

We stepped all the way into the apartment, and it was then that I saw two long picnic tables with workers bagging up dope. It was eight of them on each side of the table. On the one side they would weigh the dope, and put it into the Aluminum foil, then slide it across the table, where it was wrapped in a sandwich bag, and dropped into a Ziploc. There were platters on the tables, full of pure white Heroin. The workers wore masks, wife beaters and boxers. They moved in sync to one another. It looked like a smooth process.

Taurus pulled six bundles of hundreds out of his pockets and gave one of them to Risky. "Here, lil' bruh, this ten bands right here. I know you don't supposed to get paid until this Monday coming up, but I want you to have this because of yo' loyalty. I honor those that honor me. I ain't ever pulled up to this muhfucka without you having them hittas jump out on business. I fuck with you, man. This a token of my appreciation." He gave him a half hug and shook up with him. "And this right here is forty gees. Make sure you even it out amongst yo' killas. Let them know who my lil' nigga is and have them develop a hunger for blood over my lil' dude, because he is me. You got that?"

Risky nodded and grabbed the money from Taurus. "Just to prove it to you, I'ma make the announcement right now." He cleared his throat. "Everybody, listen up. Blades down!"

I watched as the whole room went silent. Their eyes were pent on Risky.

"Man, Cloverland is under new management. This here Shemar, and he's our boss now— certified and given his position by the homie Taurus and Hood Rich. Now, I want everybody in here to get to know the homie, so you can understand where he tryna take us from here on out. The same level of loyalty that we render to Taurus, we need to give to him also because he gon' be the one that make sure our families stay fed. You niggas got that?" he asked, looking around in anger with his all white eyes.

All around the room heads were nodding, and some looked like they were in fear of Risky snapping out, myself included. I didn't fear him, I just felt like he was a loose cannon, or unpredictable.

"Aiight, now he got a few words for us before we get back to work. Take the floor, big homie."

I took a step forward with my heart beating fast in my chest. I didn't know none of these people from Adam, and I felt real awkward standing in front of them like I was one of their own. I didn't know what they had been through together, and I kind of felt like an outsider that was calling shots over them, so I decided to make my speech short and sweet. "Look, as long as we got loyalty, we gone get rich together. This ain't about no big I's or little You's for me. I wanna see all of us eating and feeding our families. Let's hold one another accountable and to a higher standard. Be one hundred to me and the man you sitting next to, and across from you and we can have a strong family. Never be afraid to come to me about anything. We are one in the same. When I eat, so will you. You blast for me, and I'll empty my clip for you with no hesitation. Let's protect our homeland at all costs and get money."

Like I said, I wasn't looking to say much, but those lil' words must've hit every man in that room, 'cuz in less than two weeks, we were all rocking in sync and getting money.

After Taurus showed me how to work with the Rebirth, I mastered it. I found myself running back and forth between the eight buildings, getting things in order. It seemed like every time I dropped off a kilo to one building, I was picking up a bag of money at another, only to hit up Taurus for another kilo. Shit was moving so fast that I wasn't getting no sleep, and I didn't recognize it. I was falling in love with the game already. Getting money, hand over fist.

Me and Risky developed a close relationship right away. He kept tabs on the whole hood, and it seemed like didn't shit pop off in Cloverland without him knowing about it. He was like the feds. He had snitches and confidential informants everywhere. I loved how he kept his ear to the streets, and every time I rolled up in Cloverland, he met me with at least six armed men, ready to blast something over me. I couldn't understand how Flyy and Vito could fuck off a living like that. To me, Taurus was a good nigga. The way the money was coming, it was easy to become addicted to it, and lose focus if you had that Snake shit in yo' blood, which I didn't. Every time I pulled in a bag of money or dropped off a kilo, I loved Taurus and Hood Rich that much more, and I pledged my loyalty in blood to them.

One morning, after finding out where Risky laid his head, I popped up at his baby mother crib just as the sun was coming up. I was on my way to getting out of the car, when I saw the bushes next to her house move, and the barrel of a shotgun come out of it.

"Nigga, who the fuck is you!" the voice hollered.

I couldn't see the actual person, but I saw the barrel of that big boy, and it was all I needed to see before my attention was held. I didn't have a chance to respond before two other dudes slid from under cars that were parked on his block. They came up with assault rifles in their hands, beams on the top of them, and every red light was pinned on me. I felt sick.

I was scared to take my hood off of my head. "Yo', I'm here for Risky. This Shemar, nigga! Let me just pull my hood back so y'all can identify me."

They rushed me all at once with their guns pointed at me. I was thrown to the hood of my whip, then my hood was pulled back at the same time the light of Risky's baby mother's crib came on. The front door opened, and he came down the stairs just as I was poked by more than one barrel.

As he got closer, he made out my face and waved them off. "It's good, Potnas. This my nigga right here. Y'all fall back and get into position."

Slowly but surely, they let me go and went back to where they were hidden. He turned to me and helped me up. I felt like a straight lame. It was this day that made me hire my own security detail to roll around with. I didn't like how they got the ups on me. I should've had some shooters on deck that would have rivaled them, even though that would have caused an unnecessary mess.

"Boss, what brings you out to my pad, especially without giving me a heads up?" He looked me up and down.

I exhaled and tried to calm my temper. I didn't like being snatched up. "I came over here to take you and yo' family shopping, my nigga. I wanna put you in a new whip and pay up y'all bills for a few months. You know, just as a token of my appreciation."

The scowl on his face slowly turned into a smile. He nodded. "You a good dude, Shemar. I'm really good at reading niggas and I can tell that you're a really good person, but you know how this shit go when you got a woman. You can't have some other nigga coming and saving the day. If I'ma cop a new whip and bring enough money home so I can pay up the bills for six months or so, then I want her to think that I did it on my own." He looked over my shoulder at a car that rolled past. His hand going under his shirt.

The driver didn't see it, but at least ten beams were all over the car's body. Had that car stopped it would have been Swiss cheesed.

I waited for it to leave the block before I turned back to Risky. "Awright, well check this out. I got a bonus for you. Fifty gees. Do with it what you want." I opened the backdoor to my truck and grabbed out the book bag, handing it to him. "I honor yo' gangsta, my nigga."

He took the bag and exhaled loudly. "I hope I get to knock a nigga head off for you, Shemar. I feel like I just gotta show you how I get down one time, and the way the streets talking, I might just get my chance. Let's sit in yo' truck for a minute." He walked around to the passenger side and opened the door, as I sat in the driver's side. "What you know about a nigga named Yohan outta Haiti?" As he asked this, he sparked a blunt and inhaled the smoke.

I shrugged. "Taurus brought his name up a few times in passing, but I ain't got no details. Why? What's good with this nigga?" I asked, watching another car roll down the street, and once again Risky's men were all over it with their beams. The more the sun came up the less you were able to see them, but I knew what to look for, so I did.

Risky scrunched his face. "We gon' be going to war with the Zoe Pound Mafia real soon. I got word from one of the Haitians on my payroll that Taurus crossed Yohan, and Yohan is out for blood and Houston. I know how them Haitians get down and they play for keeps. We gotta be prepared to handle our business or we gon' get caught off guard."

I got to thinking about the dude Pony that we killed back in Miami. Something told me that that situation would come back to haunt us. Now it was fucked up because I was in a mind state of making money. It was a lil' hard to switch over to some war shit. I was seeing more cash than I ever had in my whole entire life, and I wanted to make so much more.

"So, what are you advising, Risky?"

He took a pull off of the blunt and held the smoke for a minute, then blew it out. "Right now, I say we keep getting money. You just let me and my niggas keep our ears to the street. We got you, but for right now I wanna employ some of my hittas to follow behind you and stay on point. I don't know where these niggas gon' splash from, but I know they coming." He frowned and sucked his teeth loudly. "I love this war shit. I'll never let a nigga out think me in my slums. Fuck that. I'd rather suck a nigga dick or somethin', and that gay shit ain't in me at all." He curled his upper lip, pulled out his phone and started texting.

"Well, you just let me know what's good. In the meantime, I'ma holla at Taurus and Hood Rich to see what the move is."

He nodded, and then a black Ford Aerostar van pulled up alongside us. The passenger rolled down its window.

"Roll yo' window down, Shemar. Let me holler at lil' fam and tell them what's good. I did just that. Risky leaned over me and hollered up at him. "This my nigga Shemar. Y'all stay close to his tail, and if anything, look fishy, wet that shit. We got some Haitian buzz coming through the area, and my nigga a target. Make sure he don't get hit. That's an order."

Chapter 9

I hustled with all of my might for the next month without no word from the Haitians. Risky had assembled a crew of savages to follow me around like I was Barack Obama or something, and I had to admit that I loved that shit. I felt like a boss. Like muhfuckas valued my life, and since all the killas that stood behind me were from Cloverland, it just made it that much sweeter to me.

After Purity getting on my nerves for damn near three weeks about not spending no time with her, I decided to take a day off from the slums to spend with her. I told her that we could go wherever she wanted to go, and I would do whatever she wanted me to do, and boy why did I tell her that? She woke me up at nine o'clock the next day, we got dressed and the first place I took her was to the Mercedes Benz car lot.

The sun was shining bright. It had to be about a hundred degrees out, and wasn't no wind blowing. I was tired from grinding so hard, and felt like I wanted to sleep for at least three days straight, but Purity wasn't trying to hear that. So, I wrapped my arm around her shoulder as we looked over a few whips.

"You know it's about time you spent some real money on me, Shemar. You always coming in the crib with bundles of hundreds and stuff. I mean, damn, don't I deserve some of that?" she asked, looking up at me. Before I could respond, she took off running across the lot. "Ooh, I want this one right here, then all you gotta do is get it custom paint, bubble gun pink, and make my whole interior Prada," she said, looking over a 2019 Mercedes Benz coupe. "It got a hard drop too? Man, I'm finna be styling." She smiled and nodded as if she was already imagining how she was gon' look rolling it.

I came over to her and looked the whip over. The sticker price was forty-five thousand, then she was talking about getting it custom designed, and I already knew I had to throw her the pink and black Faccio rims on it, so I was looking to be coming out of damn near eighty gees for Purity. I still had Simone and Nikki to spoil. I decided to mess with her. "What make you think I'm finna drop these kinda chips on you? You ain't earned this," I said, giving her a serious look.

She turned around to look up at me, searching my face to see if I was serious or not. I didn't know what she determined, but I sensed her get a little worried. "Dang, Shemar, you gon' do me like that? I thought I was your baby?" she whined, stood on her tippy toes and kissed my lips.

I pulled her into my arms and sucked all over her lips before taking a step back and smiling.

She frowned. "What you smiling for? I really want this car, and I wanna drive off of the lot with it today. Jahliya daddy just bought her a brand-new Porsche for nothin'. You out there getting just as much money as he is, so I don't understand why you ain't spoiling me like Taurus spoiling her." She wrapped her arms across her chest and attempted to pout.

I snatched her lil' ass up and bit into her neck, listening to her moan loudly before wrapping her arms around my waist. "You already know you can have whatever you want. I ain't ever finna let no nigga outshine me. If you want this Bez, we gon' cop this bitch, and I'm gon' get it custom designed for. You my baby girl, ain't that right?" I looked down into her pretty face before kissing her lips again.

"Mmm, you damn right, and can't nobody do me like you do. I mean that, Shemar. I love you so fucking much, sometimes I don't know what to do with myself."

I held her more firmly. "All you gotta do is keep going to school, getting them good grades and I'll take care of everything else. You hear me?"

She smiled and slid her tongue in my mouth while I gripped that ass. She rode off the lot with that Benz two hours later. after all of the paperwork was concluded.

After the car lot, we wound up at Sak's Fifth Avenue, where I let her go crazy. She snatched up a bunch of Prada, Gucci, and Michael Kors fits, then we shot over to the Louis store where she got her Red Bottom game up to par.

"I'm finna give Jahliya a run for her money now. I ain't gotta wear her clothes to school no more just to fit in. I can do my own thing now," she said, trying on a Dolce and Gabbana skirt.

It took all the will power that I had in me to not attack her ass while I watched her try on them fits, so before I got us in trouble, I slipped out of the dressing room and bought me a couple fits. Marc Jacobs, Robert Cavalli, Ralph Lauren, and of course I got my shoe game up to par. I was doing a lot of shopping on line for the most part, but I figured that since I was out, I might as well enjoy the shopping experience with her. In there I wound up spending another twenty bands, just on my sister. She was trying to hit my pockets like a mafucka, but it was why I hustled. As long as the women around me were happy, then so was I.

After we left Sak's, Purity wanted to cruise the city in her new whip, which I was cool with. I had my hittas following close behind us, on point, so I didn't think there was a problem with us chilling like that. We rolled around for three hours, until she got hungry and wanted to go to a soul food restaurant. So, I took her to Shante's Southern Cooking, over on Appleton Drive.

When we got into the restaurant, it was already packed, and we had to wait for about thirty minutes before a table opened up, but the food was so good there that I didn't see any problem with it and neither did Purity.

The whole time we waited in the waiting area, she was all under me. "I love you so much, Shemar, do you know that?" she asked, rubbing my face with her little hand.

I looked around and surveyed the restaurant for any type of threats. Although the place was crowded, I really didn't see any. It was mostly older couples and families with little children. "I love you too, baby. You already know you my best girl. Everything I do, I do for you first and foremost. It's always been that way. Ain't nothing changed."

She stood on her tippy toes and kissed my lips, taking her two hands and running them over my chest, but I couldn't feel it because I had on a bullet proof vest.

We made it halfway through our meal when Purity slid around in the booth and came over to my side, sucking on my neck. "You remember the last time we went out to eat, I slipped under the table and put you in my mouth? Don't you want me to do that again, baby?" She moaned, biting my neck a lil' harder.

I felt chills go down my spine. Damn, that forbidden shit was something else. Purity was driving me crazy. My dick was harder than calculus.

She reached into my lap and squeezed it. "Mmm, hell yeah, you want me to." She got ready to drop to the floor, but I pulled her up.

"N'all, we ain't gon' do that shit here. But let's go though. I want some of that pussy like a muhfucka." I paid the bill and left a healthy tip.

On the way out Shante, the owner, pulled up in her Subaru truck on her way into her restaurant, but before she walked past me, I stopped her. "Say, Shante', I just wanna let you know that I enjoyed my meal in there, and I appreciate how you run yo' business. If ever you need any help with keeping things a float, or protection, give me a call." I handed her a card with my business cell phone on it.

You see. Taurus had taught me that another rule of the game was snatching up as much support as I possibly could from the business community that surrounded Cloverland. He said that if I got them on my side it would be easier for me to clean my dirty money down the road. The key to being a King Pin was making sure that your dirty dollars had a way of becoming clean. Cash was cool, but having yo' shit in the bank was ten times better. A hustler should always prefer plastic over cash, any day.

She was a short, caramel sistah, pretty, with a nice body, and a lil' gut. She looked to be about fifty. She raised her eyebrow. "Uh, I'm sorry, but who are you?"

I extended my hand. "Oh, I'm sorry, my name is Shemar, ma'am, and Cloverland is mine."

She bucked her head and then shook it as if what I was saying made sense to her. "What ever happened to Vito? Isn't he around anymore?"

I shook my head. "N'all, the homie long gone away from here, and he's no more of your concern. I'm the man now, and I just wanted to properly introduce myself."

She sighed and looked at the ground. "So, what are you going to charge me to keep my business from being under attack, and please keep in mind that I have three children. I was paying him two thousand a week. I can do that, but please don't make me pay more than that," she said barely above a whisper.

"What?" I shook my head. "No, ma'am. I would never take your money, sistah. I'm just letting you know what it is, and as far as your business or you yourself go, if you ever have any trouble with anybody trying to shake you down, or violating your business in any way, you reach out to me, and I'll handle that, free of charge. All you focus on is strengthening your business, and pouring them black dollars into our community. God bless, sistah, and take care of yourself."

She looked at me for a long time, then down at the card that I had given her, and nodded. "You sure?"

I smiled. "Take care. You need anything, don't hesitate.

Hearing about what Vito was doing to Shante' before I took over Cloverland had me so pissed off that I could barely see straight while I sat in the passenger's seat of Purity's Benz. I hated niggas that preyed on women, especially my sistahs. There she was, trying to run a legit business in our community while taking care of her children, and this greedy ass nigga was strong-arming her. I wished that I could kill his bitch ass all over again.

I was mad all the way up into we got to the hotel. As soon as the door closed, Purity pushed me up against it, and started to take my shirt, then my vest. It dropped to the floor beside my feet, and I got to stripping her as well, and quick too. before I knew it, we were both naked, and I had her laying on her back with her legs wide open while I was eating that pussy like a Lesbian, holding her sex lips back with my thumbs, attacking that clit. Her scent was going right up my nose and driving me insane.

"Unn-a! Unn-a! Unn-a! Yes, eat me, Shemar. Eat lil' sis just like that!" She half moaned and half screamed with her mouth wide open.

I was eating that pussy like a savage, rubbing my face all in it, licking up and down her crease, sucking on her clit, and sliding two fingers in and out of her box, loving her taste. "Cum on my tongue, lil' momma. Mmm. Come on, baby. You know I love the way you taste." I started to really suck and swallow her juices then.

The aroma of her slightly sweaty pussy was driving me crazy. It wasn't nothing like the natural scent of a female to me. Pussy was the best fragrance in the world.

She humped her ass off of the bed and into my face. Her chest rose and fell while she played with her own nipples. "Uhhh! Uhh! Uhh! Shemar. Coo-a! Shit! Shit, Shemar, you finna make me cum, big bruh. I'm finna cum. Coo-a, uhhhh-shit! Unnnnnn-a!" She started to ride my tongue from her back, and I kept on licking and sucking at her clitoris, running my fingers in and out of her at full speed.

After she came, I snatched her from the bed and picked her up, making her wrap her legs around me, before sliding my dick deep into her soaking wet center. Her hot pussy slid down my muscle and I almost came in that pussy right away.

I slid her up him and slammed her back down aggressively. "Take this dick, Purity! Tell. Me. You. Love. This. Shit," I said, tossing her up and down my dick, watching her titties shake on her chest. The nipples stood erect, searching for relief.

"Uh, uh, uh, uh, uh, ooo-a, shit! Yes, daddy! Fuck me just like that! I love you so much. Uhhh! I love this diiiick!" she screamed and came all over me again.

I crashed into the wall with her and really got to fucking her hard— tossing her up and down my pipe, before falling on the bed with her. Then, I flipped her on her stomach, pulling her up by her hips, and sliding back in, slamming into that pussy like a savage. It sounded like I was slapping her on her naked back the way our skins smacked into each other. Her pussy oozed its liquids and made squishy noises. I sped up the pace and got to spanking her with my open hand.

She laid her face on the bed and got to throwing her ass back into me with a vengeance. "Uhh! Yes! Spank me, daddy! Spank me, Shemar! Hit my ass! Make me yo' bitch! Please-a!" She growled and really got to throwing her ass back.

I grabbed a handful of her hair, yanking her head back, while I beat that shit up. My dick felt suffocated in her lil' hole. I watched her ass jiggle, along with her thick thighs, and smacked her cheeks one more time before I was cumming deep within her.

Damn that shit was good.

Afterwards, I laid her on her back while I sucked on her nipples as if I were a baby, fingering her well fucked pussy.

She held her legs wide open, moaning at the top of her lungs. "You turning me out, Shemar. Makin' me crazy. You ain't supposed to do yo' sister like this. Got me gone in the head. Uhh! I'm cumming again. Oooh, I love you so much!" She screamed, and started to have a sexual seizure.

I kept on fingering her pussy until she same out of her zone.

We wound up in the bed with her crawling all over me, hugging me and kissing my chest. I could tell that she was mentally going through it. She seemed like she was in a frenzy.

"Shemar, I swear to God you're making me crazy. I can't take the way you do me, but I can't look back either. I don't want to." She kissed my chest and bit me kind of hard.

I rubbed her round booty that was in the air, sliding my finger into her crack. "What you talking about, Purity?"

She slid down my body and put her thick thigh across my waist. "I'm in love with you and I know I ain't supposed to be because of who you are, but I just can't help it. I don't want to be with nobody but you. You got me gone in the head to the point where all I think about is you, all day long. I'm obsessed with my own brother, ain't that crazy?" She kissed her way down my chest and stopped at my dick, kissing the head, before sucking it into her mouth.

I pulled her back up to me and kissed her on the forehead. "Look, all you gotta do is chill, baby. You gon' be alright, I promise you." I rubbed her back, then slid down to her ass again. I couldn't keep my hands off of that big ol' thang.

She shook her head. "N'all, Shemar, you don't understand what I'm going through. I'm ready to kill every bitch that look at you the wrong way. I don't want nobody stealing you from me. I just wanna lay up in the bed and have you fuck me all day and night long. I'll do anything you tell me to do; I swear I will. I love you that much. Don't you feel the same way, or am I kidding myself here? Am I losing my mind? Be honest." She looked into my eyes while she rubbed my abs.

As much as I didn't want to admit it, I was growing more and more crazy about her too, to the point where I didn't understand my feelings. I was wondering if we were in too deep. I had heard about other people in the south doing what we had, but I didn't know if feelings were ever developed. That was the part that scared me more than I actually realized.

I shook my head. "N'all you not losing your mind. I love you just as much as you love me, which is why I think we better pull back a lil' bit, or we gon' be in trouble. The fucking part is cool, but now that we're developing feelings and shit, I think it's turning into something dangerous, because how much further can we go without really-really crossing that line that's gon' get us in a world of trouble?"

Purity jumped up and looked down on me. "What did you just say? Did you just say we should pull back a little bit, and that the fucking part was cool?" She sucked her teeth and turned her eyes into slits. "For your information, what we do is not just fucking to me. Its more than that. Every time we connect in that way, I feel the most loved. More love than I have ever felt in my whole entire life." She looked down on me with anger and got out of the bed naked. "God, Shemar, I can't believe you make it seem like it'll be so easy for us to just stop what we're doing. I can't do that. I honestly need you more now than I ever have before. I am nuts over you, and I need you just to breathe. You control my mind, my body and my spirit. I don't want nobody else touching me if it isn't you. You're all I think about throughout the day. Before I close my eyes, I am smiling because of what we have; happy because of our special bond. Don't take that away from me just so you can give it to Simone. I'd kill that bitch before I let that happen." She slammed her fist into the palm of her hand while she paced, looking over to me every now and then.

I got out of the bed and blocked her path, trying to pull her into my embrace but she wasn't going. She pushed me away from her with anger. "Purity, chill the fuck out, baby, and let me hold you. Damn, I hate when you get to overreacting. You ain't even letting me talk." I frowned and got ready to snatch her ass up for real. Every time my sister got heated, her temper sent her on a journey that was all her own. Couldn't nobody tell her shit until she was done snapping out.

She scrunched her face and threw a pillow on the floor. "Overreacting, Shemar? Overreacting? Really? That's what you're calling this? Here I am, pouring my heart out to you, telling you how crazy I am now, and your response was to say that you think we should pull back some. It doesn't work like that for me. You're my first and only love. I've been in love with you ever since I understood what being in love meant. I don't know why I've always felt that way, but I have, and I can't help it. I just need you so fucking much, and now you're going to leave me for Simone. Why, Shemar? Why? Why can't I be your woman? You know I'll do any and everything for you. I don't give a fuck about what the world says and neither should you. Ain't I worth more than the world to you?" She was asking, walking toward me and dropping to her knees, looking up at me.

I fell to my own and grabbed her hands, looking her in the eyes. "Purity, you already know that nothing or nobody means more to me than you do. You're my everything, and you always have been." I tried to wrap her in my arms again, but she pushed me away and stood up, backing away until her back hit the wall.

She slid down it with tears coming down her cheeks. "You keep telling me that I'm your everything. Tell me that I'm your girl, Shemar. That I'm your woman, and that it doesn't matter about our relation because you and I are all that we have. Tell me that and give me a reason to live. Please!" She screamed at the top of her lungs. "I can't take this shit!"

I noticed that she started to shake. I can't even fully explain how I was feeling in that moment. I looked over at her and saw a broken little girl that had been through so much while she was away from me and in a different household. I saw a woman that I was supposed to protect at all costs, no matter what nobody said or thought. She was my responsibility. There was nothing in this world that I wouldn't do for Purity. I meant nothing. I would give her my life at the drop of a hat. So, as I looked over at her and saw how weak and defeated she was, something in me snapped, and I knew I had to be there for her by every means, and put back together the broken pieces of her. She was my baby.

I walked over to her and picked her up into the air, making her wrap her legs around me once again. Her hot box was up against my stomach, still moist from our session. It turned me on to say the least, but sex was not my motive. I held her in my arms while her face rested in the crux of my neck. Like a child,

I bounced her up and down, soothingly. "It's okay, baby. I love you. You're my only girl. My baby girl, and you're all I need. It's me and you against the world, ma. Fuck what anybody think. I belong to you and you belong to me. Do you hear me?"

She nodded. "Do you promise, Shemar? Do you promise that I'm your girl now? That you'll never change your mind or put anybody else before me? I'm not saying that I have to be your only girl right now, but I just don't want none of them other hoes on my level. I don't want you to love them like you love me. Is that too much to ask?" She whimpered into my shoulder while I continued to walk around the hotel room with her.

I shook my head. "N'all, that ain't, baby. I'll never love nobody like I love you. You're mine and I am yours. I promise."

I knew that I was laying it on kind of heavy for her, but I felt it was what she needed to hear in order to get through the moment that we were in. In all honesty, I loved Purity way more than any brother should have. I never regretted us crossing the line because of the strong love that we shared. I really didn't care what the world thought about our relationship, but it wasn't like we were gonna go promoting it either. What we had was special, and was meant to remain behind closed doors. Purity had been through so much in life and nearly destroyed by the Deacon and his family. I was her own safe haven. Her oasis, and I would be just that for as long as I had breath in my body.

She nuzzled her face into my neck some more. "Shemar, I don't want Simone to have your baby. I don't like her, and I feel like she gon' try and steal you away from me one day, and I ain't gon' take that lying down. Just like you got that animal in you, I do too."

I held her up by wrapping my arms around her lower back and waist. "Baby, what's done is done. You have to let me handle my responsibilities as a man. She'll never make me stop loving you. Nobody can do that."

"You say that now, but I'm still scared."

Ghost

Chapter 10

Over the next few months, I got to grinding so hard in Cloverland that I made my first million dollars, and I'm talking a million for me to take home and put in the safe, though by this point I was smarter than that. I'd linked up with fifteen businesses in the hood, ranging from restaurants, car washes, beauty salons, catering services, and even strip clubs, so I could launder my money. Shante had put me all the way in with the other establishments, and since I wasn't shaking them down, they were willing to help me in every way possible to turn my dirty money clean. In fact, they were making a profit fucking with me. Out of every hundred thousand that they turned over for me, I'd give them ten bands. They were happy to see a profit, and if it all fell down they would never be able to say they were forced to do anything. They were more or less accomplices, and I liked that because I didn't trust nobody outside of my circle of women, not even Taurus.

Nut set up shop in two of the buildings and brought down like twenty of his hittas from Brooklyn. These niggas looked so grimy that I didn't even wanna meet them, but Nut assured me he had them under control. I dropped him off no less than two birds a week with a street value of one hundred and fifty gees a piece because the Rebirth was so pure. That was three hundred gees altogether that I picked up every Friday. I gave him a salary of twenty gees a week, and his hittas got five every other week, and the go ahead to sell their pills and cocaine in Cloverland, long as they paid back ten percent of all profits so it could go towards the bi-weekly picnics I threw for the community.

In my second month of hustling, Shante helped me open up a nonprofit organization that catered to single mothers in our community. The program helped pay their rent, utilities, car note, put school clothes on their children's backs, and food in their stomachs. We helped the sistahs get back in school and to establish their own independence. The only criteria to become eligible for our program was that you had to be currently living in Cloverland, or trying to move into it.

Me and Nikki got an alderman to convert a few buildings into Boys and Girls clubs, and I bought two mini school buses to drive the kids around on fieldtrips, and to make sure that that they made it home safely. I was trying to do any and everything to build up my community because I knew I was tearing it down a lot. I wasn't hustling to destroy my people. I was hustling so I could get into a better position to take care of them, especially the vulnerable women and children. The more money I got, the more things started to make sense to me. I had to fully conquer the game, so I could uplift my slums.

Everything was going good for months on end. There had been no word from the Haitians though Risky kept on telling me that they were coming and I should be prepared, and I'm not saying I wasn't, but my relaxed environment caused me to become a little too comfortable, and then it happened.

I was rolling with Risky, his baby's mother, and two of his niggas. We were just coming from Harold's Liquor Store where I'd just dropped off

$50,000 for Harold to out in the bank for me. I gave him an additional five bands for himself to complete the task, and since he and my mother were on the same Chase account, I would get a text when the deposit was made.

As I was on my way out of the store, Tika, Risky's baby's mother, was coming inside of it. "Shemar, before you leave, can you snatch me up a bottle of Patron? I'll hit you back when I get some cash, homeboy. You know I'm good for it." She smiled showcasing a mouth full of gold. Tika was dark-skinned with brown eyes, and her hair was cut short into a curly style.

I waved her off and pulled out a knot of hundreds. "Stop playin' with me, you know you ain't ever gotta pay me back with no cash. Just give me a hug and let big bruh know that you love him." I opened my arms for her to walk into them.

She sucked her teeth loudly, and smiled, before walking into my arms and hugging me tightly. "I love you, Shemar. One day you gon' get me in trouble. You know my baby daddy is crazy." She hugged me for a brief second longer.

Risky walked into the store with Ray Ban's on his face. "Aw, so this what y'all in here doing while I'm out there getting baked by the sun," he joked, and walked over to us, pulling Tika away from me. "Come here, girl. You done lost yo' mind or something?" He looked down on her and I couldn't tell if he was serious or not.

Tika smiled weakly. "What? I'm just giving my brother a hug so he can buy my Patron, and a bottle of Moscato. I ain't breaking no rules, am I?" she asked, looking up at him sweetly.

Just keeping shit real, Tika was one of them fine ass dark skin sistahs that I could never help staring at. I would never cross that line with her because I respected Risky too much, but I had to give her her props. I had always liked females that were darker than me.

Risky put his arm around her shoulder and shook his head. "N'all, you good. I was just fucking with y'all. But, Shemar, you betta keep yo' light-skinned, pretty boy ass away from my woman before we have some issues. This my life right here. Only a woman of her caliber can keep a nigga like me faithful."

I smiled. "Roger that, my nigga."

Then, I turned and ordered the bottle of Patron and Moscato from Harold. While he was ringing me up, I noted that he kept on looking real nervous, and sweating way more than usual. That started to fuck with my senses. I looked over my shoulder at Risky and saw that him and Tika were tonguing each other down. When I turned to look back at Harold, his eyes got big and then he ducked down behind the counter. When he ducked down, two masked niggas with real long dreads jumped up with Shotguns in their hands.

"Fuck, Risky it's a hit!" I dropped down to the floor right underneath the counter.

Bloom! Bloom! Bloom! Bloom! Bloom! Bloom! Bloom! The shotguns spit again and again.

One of their many bullets slammed into Risky's chest and knocked him backwards into the potato chip rack. "Awww-fuck!" he hollered, falling on to his side.

I watched Tika run for the door and then the back of her head exploded. *Bloom! Bloom! Bloom!* Another bullet slammed into her back, and another into her neck before she hit the ground in a puddle of her own blood. I felt sick to my stomach.

I pulled out my .9 millimeter and aimed at the counter that I was ducking under, trying my best to hit one of the shooters. *Boo-wa! Boo-wa! Boo-wa! Boo-wa! Boo-wa!* My bullets chopped into the liquor bottles behind them, causing them to explode all over the shooters. Then, our own hittas ran into the store with their guns blazing. *Boom-boom-boom-boom-boom-boom-boom-boom-boom!* Again, and again their guns burst, chopping down the shooters that had caught us off guard. Smoke and debris flew into the air, only to come crashing down.

Errrrr-uh! A car slammed on its brakes outside of the store, then the gun shots sounded. Bloom-bloom-bloom-bloom-bloom-bloom!

One of our hittas was caught from behind. "Ahhh!" He fell forward and landed on his face, shaking while a pool of blood formed under him.

I let loose. *Boom! Boom! Boom! Boom!*

They returned their fire, getting down on one knee, aiming to kill. *Bloom! Bloom! Bloom! Bloom! Click! Click!* The three shooters got up to run out of the store when our van of hittas pulled up and let their assault rifles scream. *Doom-doom-doom- doom-doom-doom!* "Bitch as niggas!" *Doom-doom-doom-doom-doom!*

While they were handling their business, I jumped over the counter and pulled Harold up by his collar. "You bitch ass old man. How dare you set me up like that? Take me to the back and give me the disk of this shootout!" I tossed him in front of me. More and more gunfire ensued behind us. I ducked down when a bottle of Seagram's Gin exploded right by my head, before our hittas returned gunfire rapidly. Harold fell onto his stomach, and I snatched him up by his gray afro. "Get yo punk ass up, now, nigga!"

He made it to his feet and held his arms in the air. "Shemar, I swear I didn't have nothin' to do with this, man. They just came in earlier, said they knew you'd be stopping by to make a drop off, and that I'd better go through with the deal. I didn't know what to do other than follow their demands," he said, walking into the office door.

I grabbed him by the back of the neck and threw him into his desk. He crashed into it with a loud bang, and made the laptop fall on the floor. "I don't wanna hear that shit. Pop out that DVD so I can get the fuck out of here. Hurry up!"

He damn near broke his legs following my orders. I looked onto the screen from the live feed of the front of the store and saw our hittas helping Risky to his feet, while two others carried Tika's dead body out of the store. Once again, I felt sick to my stomach. They had three children together. She was a good girl, real stomp down for Risky. She would definitely be missed.

Harold popped the DVD out and gave it to me. "Here you go, man. That's the only one I got. You can have it and I ain't gon' say nothing. I swear to God." He held his hands in the air with his knees knocking into each other.

I took the DVD and slid it into my pants' pocket, then put the barrel of my gun to his forehead. "Bitch nigga, open the safe and give me my money back, now!" I ordered, pressing it harder into his skin.

He shook his head. "They took it. They took everything, even got my banking information, and your mother's too. I'm so sorry, Shemar. It was nothin' that I could prevent." Tears fell down his cheeks.

"Bruh, let's go! I hear the police somewhere down the street! We gon' meet you in the alley," one of my hittas yelled down the hallway that led to the manager's office.

My mind got to spinning so fast that I couldn't think straight. I had a big dilemma on my hands. Before I could think things through thoroughly, I smacked Harold with the pistol in the mouth, and watched him fall in what seemed like slow motion. As he was falling, I aimed straight for his head. *Boom! Boom! Boom!* The bullets ripped into his face and left him twisted on the office floor.

I broke out of there and kicked open the back door to the liquor store and took off running down the alley toward Carling Drive. I didn't get half way down the alley before Risky and our crew pulled up in my truck. I jumped in and we smashed straight to the hospital.

"She can't be dead, man. My baby can't be dead. Ahhhh! I'ma kill them bitch ass niggas!" Risky hollered, hugging Tika's lifeless body in his arms. He was covered in blood.

I could smell the stench of death on Tika. It made the hairs on the back of my neck stand up. I felt sick to my stomach, like I wanted to vomit or something. "Risky, calm down, man. Its gon' be okay. We gon' get them niggas, man. You already know we are." Just then, my phone buzzed. I looked at the face and the message was from Tez. It said that they were under attack back at the buildings, and to come fast with fire power. I felt like I was in a pinball machine, getting knocked back and forth. Now I needed to go and protect my home before it was destroyed. "Look, we gotta get back to the building. Our Brooklyn niggas under the gun right now and they need our aid and assistance," I said in a frenzy, imagining Nut getting shot down again. I mean, I knew he could hold his own, but the Haitians seemed to be coming at us real hard. I could only imagine how they were chopping down our home-front.

Risky shook his head real hard. "Fuck dat, man. We gotta get my baby to the hospital so I can save her life. What my kids gon' do? How I'm supposed to raise them without my baby, man. Dats just somethin' I can't do." He hugged her more tightly and cried harder.

Tika's eyes were wide open and unseeing. Half of her head was blown off. She smelled putrid. I wanted to tell Risky that she was already dead, but I didn't think it would help matters any because he was in his own disbelieving world.

"Aiight, well step on the gas and let's drop him off, then we gotta get to the buildings and hold our homies down."

When we pulled up to the hospital, I jumped out and opened the door so Risky could get out of it with Tika. As he slowly wiggled out of the back seat and stepped foot on the concrete, I tried my best to talk some sense into him.

"Bruh, you take her in there and they gon' snatch you up. Now, as much as I know you hate to hear it, she's dead. She's gon', big homie, and we gotta do what's smart, and the smart thing to do is to leave her in front of the hospital and storm away. Ain't nothing they can do for her right now. But her body gon' be tracked back to them murders at the liquor store. We gone be fucked, Risky. Think about." I looked around and saw an ambulance pull into the parking lot.

The medical technicians rushed out of their seats to get to the back of their truck so they could get their patient inside. All around us people were going in and out of Houston Medical. I already knew that if he got out carrying her body we would have a hundred eyes on us, and would be identified to the police in no time at all. I got worried. At the same time, I was thinking about Nut and our homies from Brooklyn. I needed to get there so I could assist him. *Fuck, Risky needed to get some common sense*, I thought.

Risky hugged Tika tightly and broke down with all of his might. "She all I know, Shemar. I been with this woman ever since I was five years old, man. This my everything, man. I don't think I can live without her. Ahhh!" he hollered and broke down all over again.

I let him cry for a full five minutes, then put my hand on his shoulder. "Bruh, let's just bury her ourselves. She gone, man. Fuck givin' her to them people. It's just gone lead back to the liquor store, then they gon' snatch all our asses up. And who gon' be there for yo' kids, man? You all they got now. Think about it," I said, watching a police patrol car pull alongside of the ambulance. "Bruh, there go the law right there. We gotta get out of here, now," I said pulling him back into the truck and reaching across him and Tika's dead body to close the door back. "Pull off, lil' homie," I ordered.

Risky cried all the way until we got to his crib. Then, I helped him carry Tika inside through the back door. Her body was already beginning to smell like burned plastic and spoiled Baloney. I was drenched in her blood. We carried her to the basement, and the last thing I saw was Risky hugging up with her. I shook my head and headed out the door.

By the time I made it to the buildings, there were so many police cars in the area that I had to keep rolling past them. They already had out the yellow tape, and I could see from a distance that there were at least nine bodies on the ground with sheets over them. Once again, I started to worry about Nut. I texted him and asked him where he was. He hit me back and said that he was at the trap over on Pike street, so I headed straight there, thankful that he was still alive.

Chapter 11

"Yo, I don't know who these niggas is, Kid, but four of my niggas from Brooklyn out there in a body bag, Sun. This is bullshit. I'm ready to flex up, my nigga. Word is bond!" he hollered, slamming a hundred-round clip into his assault rifle.

There were ten other dudes in the trap along with him, loading up weapons with mugs on their faces. I sat on the couch with my head between my legs, defeated. I didn't know what to do, and that nigga Taurus was in Paris on business. I wanted to reach out to Hood Rich, but nine times out of ten, if Taurus was out of the country then so was he. Besides, another reason I didn't wanna hit him up is because I didn't want him to think that I couldn't handle my own when I could.

Nut laid the big assault rifle on the table and loaded up another one. "All them niggas had dreads under them masks, Sun. I know it gotta be them Haitians you was telling me about, Shemar, so we finna go at they ass. My mans say they got a lil' night club over on Sycamore Street. Say they be in that bitch deep. And get this, one of the whips that's always parked in their lot came gunning at us today. A purple and black Jaguar. Ain't too many niggas in Houston rocking Jags. These niggas down here ridin' old school whips, so we sweating that bitch tonight," he growled, before snatching his mask off the couch and rolling it down his face. "You fucking with us or not?"

Under the circumstances, I really didn't have a choice now, did I?

We waited until one in the morning, right when their club was jumping before pulling across the street and looking it over closely. It had a big glass window to showcase what was going on inside. From my vantage point, I could see people in there dancing and having a good ol' time. The music was that of the Caribbean, and it was so loud that I could hear it plain as day. The entire lot was packed with Jaguars and Benz's, and the majority of them had Florida plates. The first person I thought about was Pony, then Yohan. Them niggas were from Miami, and they had finally moved some of their killas out to Houston, just like they'd been threatening to do for nearly a year.

I scrunched my face, took the grenade out of the stolen car's cup holder and jogged across the street. After pulling the pin out of it, I counted off the seconds in my head. *One... Two... Three... Four...* Then, I threw it with all of my might right through the big glass window.

Clack-tisssssh! was the sound as it broke through the glass. I ran back across the street at full speed just as Nut was making a U-turn to get onto that side of the street.

Whoooooooom! The club exploded, and then there was a bunch of screaming and people running out of it in a frenzy. We perched inside of our three vans with our beams scoping the crowd. The order was for them to only hit the niggas and anything else that looked Haitian.

As soon as the men started to run out toward their cars, we let 'em have it. *Boom-boom-boom-boom-boom-boom-boom-boom! Bloom! Bloom! Bloom!*

Bloom! Bloom! Bloom! Thot-thot-thot-thot-thot-thot-thot-thot!

I watched as our bullets ripped into the crowd, shredding them apart, knocking meat loose from faces and necks. It looked like the people were getting sprayed with water hoses the way they fell backward. Over and over again we emptied our clips and reloaded. We had to let these Haitians know that it wasn't sweet in the dirty south. I continued to scan my red beam over the crowd, picking them apart. Anything male that came into my scope, I was wetting and leaving for dead until we heard sirens and sped away from the scene.

That night, I hugged up with Purity, naked, while we watched what had taken place in Cloverland and at the club play out over the news. The reporters made it seem like Houston was under attack by terrorists. They upped the threat assessment level to red, and the city was under a nine o'clock curfew. The police were also justified and ordered to perform as many stop and frisks as they could. That made me nervous. I was worried about a loose end. Something or someone that could be tied back to me. At that time, I had a little less than two million in the bank split up between businesses, and about four hundred thousand in cash. I knew I needed to leave Houston if only for a little while, but I didn't know where I would go. I felt like my slums needed me to rid them of the Haitians.

Purity rubbed my abs and laid her head on my chest. "Damn, baby. This city is going under," she said, looking at the news and turning it to a different channel.

No matter where she turned, it was taking about the twenty people that had been gunned down at the night club, and the twelve over in Cloverland. I think we only caught one news outlet that said anything about the liquor store murders. They even had the Mayor on screen, promising to bring the culprits to justice.

My mind was reeling so fast that I couldn't calm down. I needed to take a chill pill, and the only chill pill that ever helped me was right between Purity's legs. "Look, baby, I need you to shut that TV off and get up here and ride me until I fall asleep. Can you do that for, big bruh?" I asked, rubbing her bald pussy before slipping two fingers into her center.

She moaned and opened her legs wider. "I'll do anything you tell me to do, daddy. You know I'm your slave and this body belongs to you. Umm-a." She straddled me, grabbed my dick and slid down on it, taking me whole, before riding me with a nice speed. Her titties were bouncing up and down on her chest. Her thighs were jiggling and shaking.

I loved how thick Purity was. I could never get tired of her body, and her pussy was so hot that it scalded me. I think the fact that she was fucking me made her insides warm up more than they ever did before. That forbidden sex was the greatest.

She bounced up and down on me like a bouncy house, moaning and groaning at the top of her lungs while I pulled her nipples. "This my dick. This my dick. Uhh! Shit! This my dick. I love it. I love it. I love it." She screamed as I watched my dick go in and out of her fat pussy that oozed her juices.

I could no longer deny it. I was growing obsessed with her body. It was getting to the point that I needed it every single day. Sometimes twice and three times a day, and it still wasn't enough. Her scents, her taste, her feel. I was obsessed with it all.

In the midst of our fucking, my phone started to vibrate like crazy. I sat up and held her against my chest while she continued to ride me like a porn star. Purity was figuring her sex game out and mastering that shit. I didn't wanna answer the phone, but due to what I was up against I had to see who it was, and what was going on.

"Shemar. Shemar. Unnn-a! Shit. Put. That phone. Uhhh-a! Shit! Down. Please, baby!" She moaned while rolling her hips. Her pussy was eating me alive.

I felt like I was ready to cum already.

By the time she'd said that I had already read the message from Simone, telling me that she was in the ambulance, on her way to the hospital to have the baby and that she needed me there.

I know a lot of people gon' look down on me for admitting this next part, but as excited as I was about her finally baring my seed, Purity wasn't trying to let me go nowhere until we both came, and as sad as it is to admit, I didn't leave out of the house until I came in her twice, and she came on me three times, screaming that I belonged to her and only her.

On the way to the hospital, her and Nikki damn near drove me crazy, talking negative as they possibly could.

"Man, I hope this baby come out white as hell," Purity said sitting in the front seat with her arms crossed in front of her chest. "I don't want this bitch having my brother baby. Ugh, I hate this hoe." She snapped and grabbed my hand, interlocking our fingers. "Do we have to go, Shemar? Can't you just give this bitch a bag or something?" she asked in her most whiney of voices.

I shook my head. "Purity, you know I gotta handle my business like a man. N'all. Quit all that dumb talk before I pull over and make you take an Uber back home." I loved my sister but I didn't like her calling Simone out of her name. I felt like there was no need for that. Had she been anybody else, I would have slapped her in the mouth already with no hesitation.

Purity mugged me with a look of anger. "Damn, the baby ain't even here yet and you already looking to shit on me. I knew this was gon' happen." She lowered her head, then raised it and laid it on my shoulder. "I'm sorry, Shemar. Please don't love her more than me. I was just being stupid. Do you forgive me?" she asked, and I kept on driving in silence. She leaned all the way over and put her lips to my ear. "If you forgive me, I'll let you fuck me in this fat booty when we get home. I'll do anything you want me to do, and wear whatever you want. I promise." She licked my ear and sucked on the lobe, causing me to shiver.

I didn't know how Purity had managed to do it, but she had me sexually addicted to her lil' ass. I mean, every time she touched me or spoke the way she was speaking in that moment, the animal deep within me cried out for her. I couldn't help that shit as much as I tried to.

I felt her sucking on my earlobe and that caused my dick to get so hard it frustrated me. I didn't want to be in that state of mind at that time. I should have been thinking about nobody but Simone and her bringing our child into the world safely. Man, I felt so guilty.

I made her sit down in her seat by pushing her off me a lil' bit; not enough to hurt her feelings, but enough so that she got my drift. "Purity, you good. I ain't mad at you. Just stop talking like that and let me handle my business out here with her. I need you to be on yo' best behavior because you already know what it is between me and you. We talked about this already," I said, looking at my GPS. I was set to arrive at the hospital in less than eight minutes.

Purity nodded and grabbed my hand, interlocking our fingers once again. "Okay, Shemar, I'll be cool, but I can't fake the funk. I'm jealous as hell right now." She kissed the back of my hand and laid her head on my shoulder.

I smelled weed smoke coming from the back of my whip. Nikki blew a cloud in my direction and started coughing, hitting her fist on her chest, before grabbing her pink lemonade. "Y'all so damn cute, I swear." She took another pull and blew the smoke out slowly. "Look, Purity, let me tell you something. Your brother loves you to death. I ain't ever seen him let no female be all over him the way he letting you be right now, so you should just chill. Y'all got y'all lil' down low thing going on and you don't need to expose his hand because you're in too deep, and he's not that same dude that we remember. He's head of a bunch of hustlers and killas now that's watching his every move. If they peep how close y'all are, or it clicks in their brain what y'all are doing, that could mess up a lot of things for him, and ultimately us. So, I'd advise you to play your role and just enjoy him when you can. Life is short." Nikki took another pull off of the blunt, and me and her eyes met in the rearview mirror. She licked her lips and smiled, before sitting back and looking out of her window.

Purity, rubbed the side of her cheek all over my arm, then kissed my hand again. "Okay, I'll do what you're saying, Nikki, because I know you ain't gon' steer me wrong. I'll play my role as best as I can. But I'm telling the both of y'all, I'm obsessed with Shemar, and that's just the real."

An hour later, I found myself standing on the side of Simone while she pushed and pushed to get our child out of her body. I was gon' go down to the other end between her legs, but I remembered hearing somebody say something like if you ever wanted to have sex, or desire your woman after she had your child, then don't look down when she's pushing your baby out because there is a lot that goes on down there at that time. Now, I almost rolled the dice and went to that region anyway because I felt as a man I was supposed to experience it all, but Simone pulled me to the side of her and told me to give her my support, which is what I did. I stood beside her for ten hours straight, and then finally she was ready to push our child out.

I'd been wiping her face with a cool rag, kissing her on the forehead, and allowing for her to squeeze my hand as much as she needed to. I hated that she was in so much pain during her contraction. It put a lump in the back of my throat and I was wishing I could have at least split the pain down the middle with her. I wished that when a woman was going through labor with a man's baby that the man would be able to feel everything that she did, or at least that God allowed for the pains to be split down the middle. That way, you would never need a DNA test, you would know if the kid was yours by the pains you went through while your alleged baby's mother was in labor. I already know that plenty niggas ain't feeling that, so let me move on.

Our son came screaming into the world the next afternoon, right before the clock hit two. He was screaming so loud that I knew his lungs were healthy. The doctor took him away for a brief second, and then came and gave him back to Simone, after asking her if she wanted to have skin to skin contact with him right away. She said yes, and I watched her place our child inside of her sheet, naked. I ran my hand over his head that was full of curly hair and peeped that he had deep dimples just like me. That made me proud. After she held him for a second, she handed him to me and I picked him up and held him close to my heart with my shirt off.

I felt overly emotional at holding my lil' man. I felt like I wanted to break down. There he was a little version of me. Pure and free of sin. No bodies under his belt. Strong, handsome and safe with his whole life ahead of him. A life that I had to make sure was the best one I could provide. Holding him allowed me to see things more differently. I had to conquer the game and get my chips all the way up so I could find greener pastures. I couldn't look to sleep in the game, or get comfortable enough so that I was there forever. N'all, I had to stick and move. Get rich, and then find another way to invest my bread.

It was because of my son that the next morning I signed up to take business classes o line. It wasn't much, but for me it was something major because I was starting to see past the slums, and out into a world that terrified me because it was so far away from what I was used to. Mentally, before holding my son in my hands, all I saw was the ghetto. I knew that I would hustle there and eventually die there with a smile on my face. But right then, after holding him in my arms, I wanted more for myself. I wanted more for him and Simone, and the only way any of that was going to come into fruition was if I elevated and conquered my struggles.

We named him after me. Gave him my whole name and slapped a junior on the end of it. I climbed into that bed with Simone, and held her while our son nursed at her breasts. I even found the sight of that empowering for me, because here was this woman that had only hours ago given birth to my first born, and now she was feeding him and keeping him alive. Nourishing his body, and giving him all that she had to offer. She made me respect mothers so much. I appreciated Simone, and honestly started to really fall in love with her.

Later the next day, Purity and Nikki came into the room. "Dang, y'all gon' keep us out there waiting forever. I wanna see my nephew," Purity said, coming beside the bed and holding her hands out for me to hand our child over to her. As soon as I did, she put him to her chest and looked into his face. His little eyes were closed; sleeping in a faraway place. "Umm, he don't really look like you, Shemar. I guess Simone's genes dominated ours." She laughed. "You sure this my nephew, Simone? I mean, you wouldn't be petty like that, would you? You know, trying to trap my brother and all?"

Simone shook her head. "Don't start with me, Purity. I don't have the time nor the energy to go there with you. Give me my baby."

She held out her arms for Junior, but Purity turned her back on her and started to coo to him.

Nikki snickered. "Y'all crazy as hell. Purity, give that girl her baby before she has a heart attack. That ain't cool what you doing." She walked over to me and put her hand on my shoulder while we both stopped to see what Purity was gon' do.

Purity acted like Nikki hadn't said anything to her. She kept right on rocking Junior in her arms, cooing to him. "You don't want her do you, nephew? You want me, don't you? Yeah, I know. Aunty know you do." She looked over her shoulder at Simone and smiled. "Look like he over yo' ass already, girl."

Simone started to wiggle out of the bed. I could tell that she was exhausted. She looked seriously depleted. "Purity, I always try and keep the peace with you, but if I get out of this bed, I swear to God I'm gone kick yo' ass." She sat on the edge and started to fit her foot in one of her hospital slippers.

Purity turned around and sucked her teeth. "And, bitch, I know I been staying off yo' ass for my brother sake, but if you run up on me, I'm gon' fuck you up and they gon' keep you in this hospital for a little while longer. Trust me." She curled her upper lip and her face turned red. She looked like a way prettier version of my mother when she got angry when we were kids.

Simone bounced off of the bed and got ready to run toward Purity, and when she did, Purity dropped Junior on the floor and threw up her guards. "Bitch, what's happening?" She hollered.

Junior bounced off of the floor, and started to wail at the top of his lungs. "Waaaaaaaaa!" He was laid on his side with his right leg kicking like crazy.

I ran over and picked him up, while Simone rushed Purity and they got to going at it like men. By the time I looked over to them, they were both punching each other back to back. Simone's nose was bleeding, and Purity's lip was busted. She had blood dripping off of it, but it didn't stop her from holding her own.

She grabbed Simone by her long hair and flung her to the floor, before straddling her, and punching her again and again in the face with no remorse. "Bitch! I told you! I told yo' punk ass! You thought it was sweet!" More punches, then a smack.

Simone reached and grabbed Purity by the hair and pulled her down onto her side, before kneeing her in the ribs. Purity curled into a ball and Simone straddled her now, punching her again and again. "I hate you, Purity. I hate you! I hate yo' fuckin' guts bitch!"

Nikki finally pulled Simone off of her, and Purity jumped up, and started to look around the room for a weapon. Her eyes searched and searched. Her breathing labored and rugged. "I'm gon' kill you, Simone. Mark my words, bitch. I swear on all the love I have for my brother that I'm gon' kill you." She left out of the room after saying this, with Nikki following close behind her.

"We gon' catch an Uber, Shemar. I'll see you back at the mansion. I love you, bruh."

I nodded, looking my son over. He was wailing at the top of his lungs. I pushed the button and called the nurse to come in and take a look at him.

Before she came in, Simone started to chew me out with tears running down her face. "I'm not gon' go through this for the rest of our son's life, Shemar. It's not fair. I've always tried to respect your sister but she goes too far. Our son ain't even two days old and already he's been dropped. Why do we have to go through this, Shemar? Why?" She cried.

I didn't know what to say. I felt lost and outta place. The nurse came in, and we let her know what had taken place. They rushed Junior off to the emergency room, where it was found out that he was going to be okay, but they wanted us to remain there for two more days so they could keep a close watch on him. The whole time, me and Simone refused to talk to each other. I didn't know what to say to her, and unfortunately, I didn't even try. She was right, I was wrong, that's all there was to it.

Ghost

Chapter 12

We stayed in the hospital for a total of a week after Junior was born. The whole time I'd been trying to get into contact with my mother, to no avail, and that caused me and Simone to panic because it wasn't like her to just up and go missing. She'd missed the birth of her first grandchild and had not so much as reached out to us. So, after we packed up and left the hospital, I took Simone to the house that she shared with our mother. On the way there, we spoke very few words to each other.

It was a rainy day, full of lightning, and thunder rumbling in the sky. I had so many things on my mind that I could barely focus on being with Simone and our baby. There was a heavy police presence all over Houston, and the things that me and my crew did were still all over the news. I didn't feel too secure in driving around from fear of being pulled over, but by the grace of God, we made it to our destination, safe and sound, just as the rain really started to pour like a geyser.

Simone jumped out of the car and into the rain with her blue hospital top covering her head. She ran up the stairs and opened the door, and I followed close behind with our son tucked away inside of his car seat, with my jacket over the top of it.

"Whew!" Simone exclaimed, closing the door behind us as we made it inside, safe and secure. She shook out the hospital top and dropped it next to the front door. "Feels good to be home."

I was taking the wet coat from the top of Junior's car seat with Purity on my mind. She'd left me over fifty messages in the last two days, apologizing, and saying how much she loved and needed me. It made me feel some type of way. Even though she had done a bad thing by hurting my son, I forgave her, and my love for her didn't change. Deep down I knew that she was just jealous of the baby situation. She loved me so much that everybody was like a threat to her in her mind.

After I got Junior undressed, I laid him on the couch while Simone walked to the back of the house, looking as if she was ready to pass out from being so tired.

"Ahhhhh! Ahhhh! Oh my god! Ahhh! Shemar! Shemar! Noooo! Please, God, no!" She screamed, and that caused our son to start to scream at the top of his lungs while he kicked his little legs wildly.

I picked him up and rushed into the living room while he screamed in my ear so loud that it felt like my head was ringing. There was Simone kneeled in front of one of the most gruesome sights I had ever seen in my life. Our mother, the woman that had adopted me when I was only nine years old, and in jeopardy of being lost to the foster care system, was tied to a chair, with her head pulled all the way back. Her throat was slit with globs of blood running out of it. She was without a shirt, and both breasts had been cut off and placed into her lap.

As I walked closer, I saw that something was stuffed into her mouth. Tears started to roll down my cheeks right away, and then I fell to my knees, still holding my son. I landed in her puddle of blood. There was so much that it splashed upward when I fell on it. I had gotten closer to her on my knees and laid my head in her lap, right next to her breasts.

In that moment, I felt like a lost little boy. I didn't know what to do or what to think, but I needed her. I couldn't stomach my mother being gone, and not in that way. I wondered who had taken her life.

Simone was going crazy— crying so loud that I couldn't think straight. Junior kicked wildly in my arms, before she grabbed him out of them and stood up with him. I noted that she was covered in our mother's blood. She ran into the back room with Junior. "I can't take this, Shemar. I'm getting my baby out of here. I know my father did this shit. I know he did. He's the only one sick enough to do something like this to my mother!" She screamed and started to choke on her own spit.

While she got ready in the back room, I stood up and walked closer to my mother, looking her over closely while she bled. I reached and pulled what was stuffed into her mouth out, and saw that it was the Haitian flag. Written along it was the mantra, *"You're nobody until somebody kills you. It's war!"* I balled

it into my fist and hit Taurus's line.

Twelve hours later, we were back inside of Hood Rich's private jet with me snorting line after line of cocaine. I had never fucked with that shit before this day, but I needed an escape. I'd lost my mother, a woman who had been there for me through it all. The only mother that I knew. So, yeah, I was trying to get so high that I didn't feel the pain of my heart.

Taurus picked his head up from tooting a healthy line. "Don't worry, Shemar; we finna go out here to

Port Au Prince, and cause hell. If ever a muhfucka hit one of us, or anybody in our mob, it's our job to fuck them over royally." He pinched his nose and inhaled sharply. "This nigga killed yo' momma, Shemar, so now the only logical thing for us to do is to kill his. The thing about Haitians is that they are very family oriented. Their weakness is their bloodline. If ever you want to crush one of them, you start to pick apart their family structure, and that's just what we finna do."

Hood Rich came into the back of the plane where me and Taurus was. He had on some Gucci lenses that were tinted. I couldn't see his eyes, but his face was that of sympathy. "I'm sorry to hear about what happened, lil' homie, but I just want you to know that we behind you one hundred percent. Anytime you see me, and Taurus get our hands dirty, it means that it's strictly out of love. We love you, dawg." He leaned over and gave me a hug. One that I needed more than anything at that time.

My mind was completely blown after finding my mother like that. Every time I closed my eyes, her image was all that I saw. I was taking it extremely hard. I thought Simone was worse off than I was. Not only did she have to deal with the authorities questioning her five times a day for hours at a time, but she had lost the only parent that really cared about her. I did all that I could to console her, but she insisted on being alone.

I put her up in the Sybaris Hotel suite and paid up the rent for three weeks. I just needed her to get her own piece of mind and to be out of harm's way. Both Nikki and Purity said that they would keep an eye on her for me and would support her in any way that she allowed them to. I didn't know how long it would be before her and Purity was arguing again, but my sister assured me that she would behave.

As soon as the jet landed, we stepped off of it and were ushered into a Benz truck by three armed dudes that had masks that only covered half of their faces. I got into the backseat next to Hood Rich, who was busy texting on his phone. Taurus sat in the front, speaking French to the driver.

I took a deep breath and tried to mentally prepare myself for what I was faced with out there in Haiti. I knew that things were about to get real bloody, and I just had to roll with the punches. The Haitians were insane, and in order for them to honor my gangsta, I was gon' have to get just as nuts.

We pulled into a town just after nightfall. It looked rundown, and the streets were a little more than dirt roads. The truck stopped in front of a house that looked like a rundown shack. Taurus got out first, and then me and Hood Rich followed suit. The armed men got out, walking behind us, and we followed Taurus into the shack that looked like a hut on the inside. I looked around and didn't know what to think. There was a big table in the center of the room, and the floor was basically dirt. Along the walls were green chests that had *U.S. Military* written across them, and an eagle. The driver closed the door to the shack, while Hood Rich walked over and stared to pop open the chests that were filled with assault rifles, hunting knives and bullet proof vests. He threw me a vest, and I took off my shirt and slid it on, while Taurus did the same thing.

An hour later, we sat down in front of plates of Currie chicken and white lemon peppered rice. I really didn't have an appetite, so I didn't eat, but Hood Rich and Taurus tore their food up.

"Shemar, the first thing we gon' do is knock off Yohan's twin brothers that are scheduled to touch down in the States next month to oversee Texas. You see, we gotta hit this nigga where it hurt, even before we cut his head off altogether. We gon' show you how to dismantle a boss," Taurus said before sipping his wine. He had an angry look on his face that let me know he was 'bout dat life when it came to me. I had crazy respect for both him and Hood Rich.

"Yeah, I wanna slice these niggas up and send their parts over to Yohan. This fuck nigga gotta know that this shit ain't a game. You ain't 'bout to come o to our turf and body my lil' homie's mother and not think we ain't finna make shit real difficult for you. I wanna go straight to him and murk his ass, but he's protected by some real powerful men that I can't stand to cross right now. Trust me, I asked for permission to end this nigga, but we can't until the business that he got going on with the higher ups is concluded," Hood Rich said, taking his glasses off and setting them on the table next to his plate. He closed his eyes and rubbed them.

Taurus took the bottle of Merlot and turned it up. I watched his Adam's apple move up and down before he placed the bottle back on the table. "Shemar, I know you're mentally going through it. But you gon' feel a lot better once you get to killing this nigga people. I know it ain't gon' bring yo' mother back, but it's the first step to healing. Being in this game, you gon' lose a lot of loved ones. You just gotta keep on moving forward, and not let that shit get you down. Understand that it comes along with the territory. I'ma hold you down, though. The best that I can. Even killas get heavy hearts." He lowered his head and shook it.

I spent my first night in Haiti preparing to buss these moves with Hood Rich and Taurus. I couldn't quite get a hold of myself mentally. No matter how hard I tried, I broke down on the bathroom floor of our shack, missing my mother. The bathroom floor was comprised of nothing but dirt and little rocks, and as I fell to my knees, I felt the rocks digging into them, but I didn't care. I cried my heart out for the only mother that had ever gave a care about me. I missed her so much. I didn't know if I would ever be the same again. As the tears dripped off of my chin, I rocked back and forth on my knees, looking at the tin roof of our shack. Tears ran down my neck, and my heart was beating so hard in my chest that I could barely breathe. No man should ever have to lose a mother twice. It was almost more than I could stomach.

I Facetimed with Simone and my son, and it made me feel a little better. I could see the bags under her eyes as soon as she looked into the screen. Junior laid on the side of her with his eyes opened, and he had a big smile on his face. Both dimples were deep on each cheek.

"I ain't even gon' lie, Shemar, I'm at my breaking point. I feel like life is going to be too much to handle now that my mother is gone. I don't feel like I'm strong enough to handle it." She blinked and tears ran out of her eyes.

Beside her, our son continued to kick his little legs. He was yawning a lot. He really was a perfect blend of me and Simone. I would always be in debt to her for bringing him into the world. A man should never be able to look at a woman the same after she had his child. I looked at Simone as if she were a god. I appreciated her more than I even knew.

"Baby, I just want you to know that I love you, and that as soon as I get home, I'm gon' do everything that I can to build you up because you deserve that. I appreciate you, Simone. I mean I appreciate you so, so much for everything that you do, and I'm sorry that we lost or mom. I wish I could change that part, baby," I said, with my voice breaking up and tears running down my cheeks.

I missed my mother so much, and the more I looked at Simone, the more she started to look like her. It was at that point that I knew with her is where I needed to be. I was going to settle down and be with my son's mother, faithfully. I didn't know how I was going to break the news to Purity, but I knew I was going to.

Simone sniffled snot back into her nose. "I need you here with me right now. I'm not strong enough to be alone. Please, come to me, Shemar. I am begging you. I am weak, down and on my way out. You have to believe me when I tell you this." She broke into a fit of coughs that made our son start to cry at the top of his lungs. Simone looked into the camera with the bags under her eyes, and shook her head. She then pulled up her shirt, allowing him to latch on to a nipple. "When will you be back here, Shemar?"

I swallowed and exhaled. "In a few days. Once I get back to you, I promise to never leave your side again. Until then, I'ma have Purity and Nikki come over there to help you out. And don't tell me not to, because it's happening whether you want it to or not. I'm worried about you. I need you, boo."

Simone waved me off. "Even though I ain't got time to be going through that shit with Purity right now, I ain't gon' fight her helping me because I need it. Just holler at her ahead of time, and tell her to keep that bullshit to a minimum. I love you, Shemar, and I can't wait until you get back to me so we can work on being a family. I can't do this on my own. I swear I can't." More tears fell out of her eyes, as our son continued to suckle at her nipple.

"I love you too, baby, and as soon as I can get to you, I'll be there. It's time that I manned up and be everything that you need me to be for our family."

After the call with her, I felt a little better, but dreading making the next ne that was to go to Purity. I didn't know what I was going to say to her yet because I didn't exactly know where she fit into the scheme of things. As crazy as it sounds, I was more in love with Purity than I was with Simone. I craved her and found myself needing her every second of the day. I didn't want what we had to end, and I wished that I could have found a happy medium for it all to work out, but that wasn't my reality. They hated each other, and Purity was so selfish when it came to me that I already knew that sooner or later I would have to choose between the two.

I stood up and paced for a few minutes before making the call to Purity. I still didn't know exactly what I was going to say, I was just thinking that I would let things flow naturally.

She picked up on the second ring sounding like she was worried. "Hello? Shemar, tell me what's wrong. I know something ain't right because you calling me right now instead of texting me. Are you okay? Please say yes," she said out of breath. In her background I could hear the voice of SZA bellowing out of the speakers. I knew that she was one of her favorite singers.

I sat down on the broke-down toilet and closed my eyes. I felt my stomach flip over a few times, then I exhaled loudly. "Purity, I gotta be a man and step up to the plate for Simone. She has our son now, and I think it's in his best interest that me and her be together and give him the strongest foundation that we can muster. You know we never really had a father, and I don't want my—"

She cut me off. "What the fuck are you saying to me right now, Shemar? What are you doing to me?" She screamed into the phone before the sobbing started.

I felt super sick now. So sick that I started to dry heave. I never liked hurting my sister. Even when we were little kids and we'd be playing around, she'd wind up getting hurt, and seeing her crying always broke me down. I just couldn't handle it. She was my heart and soul. Every ounce of pain that she felt, I felt it ten times more than she did, or at least that's how I felt.

"Purity, please just hear me out, lil' sis. I'm not saying that I'm about to—"

She cut me off again. "I knew that as soon as this bitch had your baby that you were going to shit on me and start to second guess our special relationship. This is bullshit, Shemar, and you know it. You're supposed to love me more than everybody else in this world, just like I love you. Now that this girl done had your baby, you want to leave me out in the cold all over again. Why? Why, Shemar? Why can't we just be together and fuck what the world has to say about it?" She cried. It sounded like she dropped the phone because I heard a loud crack, and then her sobs seemed as if they were far away.

"Purity! Purity! Pick up the phone, baby, please!" I hollered, feeling a lump form in my throat. Hearing her cry was tearing me apart. I needed to heal her and fast.

I guess I wasn't as sure about what I wanted to do as I thought. I loved her way too much to allow her to process that pain. She was my little sister, and my everything. It was what it was, and I felt that I had to quit running from our reality, no matter how frowned upon it was.

"Purity! Please, baby, pick up!" I felt the uncontrollable tears slip out of my eyes and roll down my cheeks. I wished that I was back in Texas with her at that time so I could console her. I was the only person on earth that could heal her, and there I was hurting her just like everybody else. I felt like a straight bitch. "Purity!"

She continued to cry for a few moments longer, then she picked up the phone. "Hell-low." I could hear her sniffling a lot.

I ran my hand over my deep waves and took a deep breath, exhaling slowly. "Baby, I'm sorry. I'll never leave you, and you're the only one I wanna be with. I just thought that being with Simone would have been the right thing for me to do, but it ain't if it means that I gotta hurt the love of my life in the process. I'm so, so sorry. Do you hear me?" I asked with my heart beating fast. I held my breath while I waited for her response.

"Shemar, you have no idea how much I love you. I just can't be with anybody else. You're the only person in this world that I care about. We've been through so much heartache and pain. Why is it so wrong for us to just be together, happily? Fuck the sibling thing. The world is going to judge us for something else if it's not that anyway. So why not live life with our eyes trained on each other? At the end of the day, it's all that really matters." She sniffled and exhaled loudly.

I was just happy that she was talking again and not breaking down like before. I couldn't take hearing her in that state of mind. As far as everything else she was saying, I wished that it could have been that simple, but it just wasn't. By us trying to be together, we would be faced with so many obstacles that in all actuality we would never be allowed to be happy one hundred percent. But, I couldn't lie about how much I loved her and needed her in the same way that she needed me, if not more. I just didn't want to do the wrong thing.

154

I had to do right by Simone, but at the same time, I didn't want to do wrong by Purity, so I was stuck in a space that had me literally sick. It felt like whoever I was with at that moment was who I felt the most understanding and love for, but honestly, underneath it all, Purity had my heart.

"Baby, I don't know what the future holds for us, but one thing I do know is that I love you, and I'll never leave nor forsake you. You have my word on that. When it comes to Simone, we have to figure out a plan that works for her and my son as well.

We can't just kick them to the curb. You hear me?"

She was quiet for a little while. I could hear SZA still singing in the background. "Shemar, you don't worry about Simone. By the time you get back here, me and her will have a good understanding. I'm on my way over to where she is right now."

I nodded, hoping that they would be able to get along for a change, at least until we all figured things out. "Do you promise me that you'll do your best to be cordial toward her?"

"With all my heart."

Ghost

Chapter 13

The lights flickered on and off inside of the warm living room. All of the windows were covered by black blankets that Hood Rich had put up. Where he'd got them from, I had no idea. I stood in front of Yohan's brother, along with his brother's wife, while they were tied to a chair by Taurus. In my hand was a serrated Army knife that I held firmly. I looked the man in the eye as sweat poured down his face. His wife to the left of him hadn't stop crying ever since we'd snatched her from the bath room, fresh after her shower.

Taurus walked up to the dread headed man and stuffed a white towel in his mouth so far that he started to gag. His wife's mouth had been duct taped shut. Snot dripped out of her nose and over the tape. I was trying my best to not feel so sorry for her. I tried to imagine my mother and what she must've felt as Yohan's crew murdered her in cold blood.

Taurus kneeled into the dude's face. "You know why you here, Fuck Nigga?" Taurus grabbed him by the throat and looked into his face closely.

He shook his head. "Ummm-ummm!" He looked like he tried to get up, but couldn't because Taurus flung his ass back down to his chair.

"Well, since you don't know, I'm just gon' tell you. You're here for the sins of your brother Yohan. Since right now he's untouchable, you're going to have to be his sacrifice. I'm gon' enjoy this shit," he said standing up, and patting me on the back. "Go ahead. Handle yo' business, lil' homie. Wait, let me turn this nigga in front of his bitch so she can see this shit in real time." He moved the dark-skinned dude's chair until he was nearly face to face with his wife, just leaving enough room for me to be able to get into so I could do my thing.

I gripped the handle of my army knife hard, stepped in front of him, cocked back and slammed the blade into his chest with all of my might. The blade sunk in before I pulled it out and slammed it into him all over again, taking pleasure in feeling it break through his rib bones. I was envisioning my mother in my mind, imagining him and his brother taking turns killing her. I felt tears wanting to leave my eyes under my mask, but I held them back and focused on my arm going back and forth, stabbing him again and again.

Oof! Oof! Oof! Oof! was the sound the knife made as it entered his body repeatedly. He wiggled in the chair and screamed into his duct tape. "Hmmmm! Hmmmm! Hmmm!" Blood gushed out of him every time I pulled the knife out of his torso.

His wife was shaking so bad that the legs on her chair was knocking against the floor. She soiled herself, lowered her head, and I could hear her mumbling under her duct tape, probably saying some sort of prayer. Once again, I tried my best to not feel sorry for her, but I was finding it hard.

After I was sure that he was finished, I took a step back and looked over my work. Yohan's brother lay slumped over, bleeding profusely. He smelled like bile and piss.

Taurus walked up to him, looked down and smiled. "That's a dead nigga right there." He started laughing, and so did Hood Rich.

Hood Rich walked over to the dude's wife and yanked her head back by her long dread locks. "Slice this bitch throat, lil' homie. Ain't no love for these punk ass Haitians. Trust me, they'll kill every female in yo' household, and I wouldn't be surprised if they didn't send her to pull the trigger. Your heart gotta be cold when it comes to this game. Now, slice this bitch throat."

"Unnnn! Unnn! Unnn!" She screamed and started to shake her head from side to side, even though Hood Rich was holding her by her dread locks. She kicked her legs wildly.

Taurus walked up to her and leaned down. "I think she trying to tell us something, bruh. Hold on." He snatched the tape off of her mouth while the lights continued to flicker on and off in the background.

The stench of her dead husband was getting to my stomach. Not enough to make me feel sick but enough to let my body know I was inhaling something toxic.

"Bitch, what you tryna say?" Taurus hollered into her face.

She jumped back into Hood Rich. He tightened his grip on her dreads. "Please. Please, don't do this. I'm not responsible for what my husband does. I'll give you one million Euros if you let me live." She whimpered with snot pouring out of her nose.

Taurus turned around to look at me. "This bitch think it's about the money. Okay, so let me see what she getting at." He turned back to her. "Where is this million at, lil' lady, huh? What? You gotta go to the bank or somethin'?" He laughed to himself, but I could tell it wasn't one of them goofy laughs, but one that natural born killas made before they bodied you.

"In my son's bedroom closet. His wall, it pushes in. There's one million Euros, and five hundred thousand US dollars. You can have it all, just leave me with my life. I'm all my son has. He gets home from school in an hour." She whimpered with tears rolling down her cheeks.

Now I was really feeling sorry for her and I hated myself for doing so. I didn't think that she should have been held responsible for the sins of her husband and his brothers. I felt that she was going to suffer enough by being a single mother. We'd just taken away her bread winner, I assumed, and for me I felt that was enough because we were still going to kill his brother, and some more enemies before we left Haiti.

Hood Rich let her hair go a little bit. "Which room is your son's, and you bet not lie. If I go in there and don't find no money, we gon' have a problem." He pushed her head into her lap and waited for her response.

She turned around and pointed at a room, before Hood Rich took off in that direction. "All I want is my life. I don't want any trouble with you Americans." She rolled her head around on her shoulders.

Taurus shook his head. "You lucky everybody got a price, because if they didn't, you'd be out the game already."

"Aiight! I see the closet she talking about it. Which way do I push or pull this wall, bitch!"

She sat up in her chair. "Do you see a red coat that's hanging up?" She yelled in a heavy French accent.

He was silent for a moment, then he must've found it. "Yeah, I see it! And what?"

"Well, you move the coat to the side and push on the wall real hard. It's going to open." She lowered her head and started to mumble under her breath with her eyes closed.

I noticed her shaking and everything. I wanted to get the fuck up out of there. I didn't think we needed to kill this woman because it would serve no purpose, and I was gon' tell Taurus that just to see what he said. I stepped to the side of him and leaned into his ear. "Say, Taurus, I think we should just let shawty—"

Boooooooooom!

The room exploded into a ball of fire, picking me up off of my feet and throwing me against the wall, knocking the wind out of me. "Aww fuck!" I hollered, reinjuring my shoulder somewhat. I tried to breathe and was having a hard time doing so. My eyes were bucked, and the smoke caused me to choke.

Hood Rich ran out of the room on fire. I'm talking fully engulfed in flames. It looked like he was walking in slow motion. "Ahhh! Ahhh! Fuck! This punk ass bitch!" He fell to the floor and started to roll around on it, sizzling like a piece of bacon while I tried to breathe.

The woman had fallen onto her side and somehow managed to slip out of her tape. She got to her feet and ran to the front of the house, and disappeared in the smoke while Hood Rich screamed at the top of his lungs, slowly dying on the floor.

Taurus got to his feet, staggering. He got over to Hood Rich and looked down on him. By this time, his skin had melted off of his bones as if the closet had been booby-trapped with some kind of gas bomb. The way his skin melted away so fast proved that it had to be something like that.

"Kill me, Taurus! Kill me! Please, bruh! Ahhhhh! Ahhh!" he hollered, smelling like fried pork.

Taurus kneeled and crossed himself with the crucifix, then pulled out his .9 millimeter. Boom! Boom! Boom! "Let's go, Shemar, hurry up!" He grabbed my hand and pulled me toward the back of the house where we'd parked his Jeep.

As soon as we got outside, there was a crowd of people surrounding in the back of the house. We ran past them just as another Jeep rolled up with three heavily armed men in fatigues. Taurus got to the Jeep and threw open the door, while I beat on the window of the passenger's side before he popped the lock.

Boom! Boom! Boom! Boom! Boom! Boom! Boom! Boom! Bullets came flying into our direction, slamming into the body of the Jeep just as Taurus got it started and skirted off.

"Duck yo' ass down, Shemar! These Haitians play for keeps! I don't know how we finna get out of here," he said, stepping on the gas and hitting a man that was trying to get out of the way.

Whoom! Then I felt the Jeep rolling over his body. I looked behind me to see him jump up and fall back down to the ground only a few steps later. Two

Jeeps got behind us, with armed men using us as target practice.

Boom-boom-boom-boom-boom-boom-boom-boom!

A few of the bullets slammed into our windshield, shattering it into our laps. I ducked and felt my heart skip a beat. I felt like in any moment I was about to be hit by their gunfire.

Taurus drove with his head down, flying down a dirt road before turning into a wooded area. "Shemar, our only hope is to get on the eastside of the island. That's where I got a few connects. If we stop, they gon' kill us, lil' homie. Fuck, we shoulda never trusted that bitch!" he growled, making a strong left so hard that the Jeep almost flipped over.

It balanced itself on two wheels before falling back down. I looked over my shoulder and saw the Jeeps still following us close behind.

Boom-boom-boom-boom-boom-boom-boom-boom-boom-boom-boom-boom!

Ca-szzzzzz! One of the tires had been hit, causing the Jeep to waddle from side to side.

"Fuck, Shemar! Them bitch ass niggas!" he said, not taking his eyes off of the road. He stepped on the gas and shot out of the woods onto a busy street, side swiping a car before jumping the curb and crashing into a fruit stand full of watermelons. The air bags deployed. He opened his door. "Come on, lil' homie, before they cross that street." He waited for a brief second so I could get out of my side, before we took off running at full speed.

I looked over my shoulder one time and saw the Jeeps waiting for their turns to cross the busy intersection, before I was running behind Taurus, praying that he knew where he was going. We ran into a restaurant, scaring the shit out of the patrons, all the way through the dining area and into the back where the cooks were serving up the platters. I felt my lungs getting tight, but Taurus looked like he could run forever. I was about to stop and take a break. Fuck that. I could barely breathe.

Taurus knocked over a cook, then pushed the dishwasher out of the way, before we hit it out of the backdoor and into an alley that was mostly another dirt road. By the grace of God, some older man was just then pulling up on his Moped, but he never got the chance to park because Taurus clothes-lined his ass off the bike, before picking it up and running a little bit with it.

"Come on, Shemar, get yo' ass on!" he hollered.

I waited for him to get situated, and then I got on right behind him. He revved the engine and pulled away, sending dust into the air.

We didn't make it more than two minutes away from there before we were back in the woods, traveling down a path that looked foreign to me. When we came to a little creek, Taurus stopped the bike, and we got off of it, and my eyes got bucked as hell when I saw him walk into the water as if it was the most natural thing in the world. I stood on the bank, looking down on him like he was crazy.

He turned around to see me not following him. "Shemar, what the fuck! Let's go!" he ordered.

Before I could even think about the fact that I didn't know how to swim too ineptly, I jumped in and followed close behind him, feeling the seaweed wrap around my legs and ankle. I was freaking out already, not knowing what to expect. The sun had gone completely down, so I couldn't see in front of me enough to feel secure. I was panicking way more than I really wanted to admit.

"Shemar, alright look, you gotta dunk yo' head under water, and to our left gon' be this lil' cave. We gotta swim through it for about a minute, then, once we come up, we'll be in safe territory. I been through it before, and Hood Rich told me that if ever I got in trouble that this is where I had to go!" he hollered over his shoulder at me.

I was about to become hysterical. Now he was talking about going under water and swimming for a full minute. I didn't think I could do that. I was freaking out so bad that I was worried about having a heart attack. "I can't swim, bruh. What the fuck I'ma do?" I yelled with the murky water up to my neck, still following behind him.

A Jeep rolled up on the bank. I could see the lights from the front of it, then I heard the doors open, and heard a bunch of boots on the grass. There was murmuring.

"Look! There!"

Boom-boom-boom-boom-boom-boom! Pee-yon! Pee-yon! The water splashed up every time the bullets sliced through it.

Taurus grabbed my head and dunked me under after saying, "Just hold on to me, lil' bruh. I got you!"

The bullets continued to rip through the water as we dropped beneath the surface. I was holding my breath and my nose at the same time, swimming like a first grader. I could feel Taurus pulling me forward while I kicked my legs. We bumped into something hard, for a second, then swam to our left, and proceeded to swim through the cave-like area. It felt like it was no wider than the width of my body, which caused my claustrophobia to kick in. I opened my eyes under water, but I couldn't see anything. That made me even more scared. I was praying that Taurus knew where he was going and that we got there real soon because I was running out of breath. My heart was beating fast. My lungs were getting tight and feeling like ice were inside of them.

My throat had so many lumps in it that I felt like it was about to burst or something. We swam and swam, and then Taurus stopped for some reason, and the only reason I could think of was that he was lost, and that made me really panic. I couldn't hold my breath any longer. My heart started to pound in my chest. I kicked my legs, and then I fucked up and did the goofy.

I opened my mouth and inhaled so much water that I started choking. Taurus tried to grab a hold of me but I was panicking. Then, he started to move all crazy like. There was no air and no end to the cave in sight. I swallowed a few more ounces of water and then I felt my chest burst before everything faded to black.

I don't know how it happened or when, but I do know that my mother must've been protecting me from heaven because when I opened my eyes, I was back on Hood Rich's plane, and there was a fine ass Jamaican sistah sitting on the side of me. I had an oxygen mask over my face, and she rubbed my chest repeatedly. My head was pounding like an 808 drum.

Taurus came and looked into my face. "Shemar, you a lot of thangs, but a swimmer ain't one of them. I'm glad to see you made it, doe, lil' homie. You had me a lil' worried. We got too much business to handle, especially now that Hood Rich out of the picture." He shook his head and picked up a bottle of Moet, sipping from it.

The Jamaican sistah continued to rub my chest. "Yurr okay now bay-be. Don' chu worr-we nun. Ya ear me now?" She asked and leaned over to fidget with the oxygen machine. Her plump titties jiggled in my face. I could see the indentation of her nipples through the white uniform top that was unbuttoned nearly to her stomach.

Taurus sat down on the seat across from where I was laid out. "Shemar, once we get back to Texas, I'ma give you a lil time to get yo self together, then we gotta get right on business. The streets saying them Haitians trying to take over Houston. Our troops been at war with them ever since we left. Now that Hood Rich gone, I gotta make some power moves up top. You and Risky gotta get our slums in order. It's for you to be the new me since I gotta step into Hood Rich's shoes. Life about to speed up a hundred miles an hour for us, and we gotta be ready to handle that shit."

I didn't know what to say because I still felt so damn dizzy. My chest was killing me, and all I could think about was the fact that I was still alive.

Ghost

Chapter 14

Nikki sat on the couch with her head down, shaking it. It was two days after Hood Rich's murder, and I'd returned home to find out that Cloverland was under intense pressure, not only from the Haitians but the law enforcement as well. It wasn't safe to drive through the city as a black male without getting pulled over and pulled out of your car. Then, the police would whoop your ass and take you into the station just because. The curfew was at six o'clock now. Anybody caught in Houston after that time was at risk of being hauled into the police station.

Nikki stood up and exhaled loudly. "Nut gotta be dead. I'm tellin' you. I sat there and watched him take about six slugs to the chest. Them Haitians ain't playin' no games. Had I not drove away when I did, I would have gotten popped up as well," she said, pacing in front of me at her crib.

Purity walked over and sat on my lap, holding my face between her small hands, then kissing me on the lips. "I'm so scared for you to be out there now. If the niggas don't get you then the police is. I think we should just leave Houston and go somewhere else." She kissed my cheek and wrapped her arms around my neck, laying her head on my chest.

Nikki looked at her then rolled her eyes. "I don't know what we should do, Shemar, but she does have a point. It really ain't shit here for us no more. We're super-hot, especially you. Oh, and did you know that Tim got killed yesterday on Foster Road?" She bucked her eyes and looked me over closely.

I shook my head. "N'all, I ain't know that, but I really don't care. That lil' nigga was super shiesty. Sooner or later, somebody was gon' clap his ass. I ain't got no time to be worried about his murder. I need to know what's good with Nut." I sent him another text, telling him to pick up his phone. Then, I said fuck it and called his line.

It rung eight times, and then somebody picked up. It sounded like a white man. "Hello? Somebody calling Terrell's phone?" came the voice.

I scrunched my face. "Yeah, and who the fuck is this?" Nikki ran over to me and tried to take the phone out of my hand, but I held it away from her. "Move, I'ma put it on speaker so you can hear too. It sounds like a white man or something."

I switched the phone to speaker. "Hello, did you hear what I said?"

"Loud and clear. This is Federal Agent Wilson, and I want to inform you that Terrell has been taken into custody. I take it this is the mighty Shemar Stevens?"

I dropped my phone on the floor as I felt my heart leap out of my chest. It seemed like everything started to move in slow motion.

Nikki walked over and picked the phone up. "What has Terrell done? Why are the feds fucking with him?" she asked, mugging the phone. She started to pace all over again.

I could tell that she was worried because it showed in her face.

Purity jumped up and tried to take the phone away from Nikki. "N'all, Nikki, y'all should throw that phone away. They could be tracing that call," she said and reached for it.

Nikki moved it away from her again. "Fuck that! We ain't did shit and ain't got nothing to hide. Fuck this white man! Why you snatch Terrell?" She screamed.

"You must be Nicole Wilson. Um, um, um. You're in so much trouble, little lady. Your time is running out."

Nikki froze and looked down at the phone. "What did I do?" she asked with her voice breaking up.

He laughed. "Where do I begin? How about five counts of murder, one robbery, home invasion, the sale of narcotics, and the list goes on and on. We've been watching you and Shemar for a very long time. You're done unless you give us Shemar. And Shemar, you're done unless you give us Taurus and Hood Rich. Ahh. We got all of you by the balls, even you, Nikki. I mean, you do still think you're a man, right?" He laughed again, this time at the top of his lungs.

I snatched the phone out of Nikki's hand and slammed it on the floor. "Look, we gotta get out of here. If the feds on us like this, we gotta move!" I felt dizzy as hell. Panic was starting to set in once again, and I didn't know what to do. I had to get word to Taurus. I had to let him know what was going on.

Five minutes later, we jumped into the pink Mercedes Benz that Taurus had bought Nikki. I sat in the passenger's seat with it all the way back. I had so many things going through my mind that I was getting a migraine. You see, at that time I really didn't know how the feds worked. Growing up in

Cloverland, you heard about the older hustlers getting indicted all the time, and that was supposed to be the one fear of being in the game.

It was blowing my mind that they knew so much about me and Nikki. I didn't even think they clocked females like that, so my head was spinning.

My phone buzzed and I looked at the face to see that Risky was sending me a text. It said that he needed me to meet him over at Jim's Pawn Shop over on Baker Road. He said that it was urgent. I texted him back that I would be there in an hour, but to be honest, at this time I really didn't want to go. I needed to take some time to myself just so I could clear my head. I needed to get into contact with Taurus too, but that caused me another dilemma because I had already crushed one of my phones because the feds popped up on it. I had one left on my hip, but I figured that that one had to be hot as well, and if mine were hot then I knew that Nikki's two were blazing because they seemed to be tracking both of us. I exhaled loudly and shook my head.

The sun was shining so bright that I had to squint my eyes. It was humid and it felt like I had two sweaters on under my vest, and I didn't.

Purity reached from the backseat and rubbed my left shoulder. "Shemar, are you okay up there? I'm worried about you because you've been quiet ever since we left Nikki's crib. What are you thinking?" she asked.

I shook my head and lowered it. "Purity, right now I'm just a little lost. If these feds been jocking us like this, then I'm just wondering how much do they really know. I done did some shit over the last

172

few months. I ain't trying to see that needle. Fuck that."

I knew that in the state of Texas that they were quick to put a nigga on death row, before pumping you full of that poison. I was just eighteen years old. I wasn't trying to be on death row or doing no life sentence in nobody's prison. I'd rather hold court in the streets and let the cards fall where they may. The only thing that was killing me mentally was the fact that once they did whatever they were going to do to me, neither Purity, Simone, or my son would have anybody to protect them. They would wind up being in this world all alone and defenseless. That made me want to break down to my knees because it was my responsibility to protect them and provide for them at all costs.

I felt Purity squeeze my shoulder a little harder. "You're making me scared now. Do you think they're going to try and take you away from me? Like lock you up for a long time or something?"

Nikki sighed. "I sho' hope not. Before that shit happen, Shemar, let's just get the fuck out of here. We can go fuck with my people out in Brooklyn, or Virginia, and lay low. The feds only on us like they is because Cloverland burnt the fuck up. We gotta get up out of here like ASAP. I'm talking tonight. What's good?" she asked, looking back and forth from me and then the road.

"Yeah, Shemar, let's do it. I mean, I can come too, right, Nikki? You already know I ain't about to leave him under no circumstances because I'd rather die first."

"Ain't nobody finna die, Purity. You already know if I'm going anywhere then you coming, too. I can't be away from you. You're my baby girl. Nikki know what's good," I said smiling.

Nikki frowned and then smiled slowly. "I know one thing, if we do head out east, all that fucking and shit y'all doing, I'm climbing in that bed with y'all. Shit, we can have a real family affair. He ain't the only one that's trying to be all over you, Purity. I done watched yo' lil' ass get thicker than me. I definitely wanna know what that's like down there." She ran her tongue across her lips and looked in her rear-view mirror, I guessed making eye contact with Purity. "You got a problem with that back there?"

I turned around so I could see Purity's response. I hadn't ever heard about her messing with no females before, so I was curious as to what she was going to say.

She looked into my eyes. "I'll do whatever Shemar want me to do because I'm his property. He runs this right here, and if he wanna see our thick asses rolling around in the bed while he does whatever he wants to, to the both of us, then I'm with it. Just as long as he don't love you more than he does me, I'm good. Nikki, you been fine to me, and you're just as strapped. I be peeping yo' booty, I can't lie." She bit into her bottom lip all sexy like, and looked me back in the eyes.

Nikki kept rolling. "Shemar don't love nobody more than he loves you, but he does love me too, so don't get to acting all crazy when we get over there. Just know that I love both of y'all, and y'all are the only brother and sister that I have. If I'm gon' lay in the bed with anybody, giving them all of my love, it's gon' be one or the both of y'all." She pulled up at a stop light, leaned over to me, grabbed me by the back of the neck and we started tonguing each other down like savages.

I tasted her peach lip gloss and tried to suck it all off of her lips. I loved hearing her moan into my mouth. It drove me crazy. Nikki was something else.

Purity leaned forward in her seat and wrapped her hand around the back of my head before joining the kiss with me and Nikki.

I sucked on her lips, then she sucked on Nikki's, and they tongued each other for a long time before I felt Nikki's hand in my lap, grabbing my dick and squeezing it. I slid my hand right up her short Prada skirt, playing all over her bald, fat pussy lips, trying to slide a finger in her. She opened her thighs wide and slid her hand into Purity's blouse while they started to tongue each other down again. There was so much moaning and heavy breathing jumping off that I felt like I wanted to fuck.

We didn't get snapped out of our zone until a car behind us blew its horn. By that time, everybody was highly aroused.

"Look, I say we shoot out to Brooklyn, while at the same time seeing if Virginia is a good fit. Me and Purity got some cousins in both places, and I got a little more than two million put up in cash, not to mention the bank accounts. That's a little more than that. I just gotta get in touch with Taurus to let him know what's going on, and we'll go from there."

"Man, that sounds good. I can't wait to get the fuck away from here. Oh, wait a minute," Purity said.

She sighed. "What about Simone? Do she gotta come?"

Nikki pulled onto the highway and looked over to me with her eyes wide. "Damn, I forgot about ol' girl and the baby. What we gon' do about them, Shemar? You know she ain't finna gee for the arrangement that me and Purity proposing."

I smiled. "I'm way ahead of you. That's why I'm thinking we fuck with Virginia too, because I want us to grind out in New York and I'll have my lil' family out there in Virginia. No harm, no foul, right?"

Both girls were quiet and avoided eye contact with me for the rest of the ride. I wanted to know what was on their minds, but I refused to ask because their silence told me everything that I really needed to know.

Fifteen minutes later, I sat on the edge of the bed of the hotel I'd had Simone stay in while I was getting things in order.

She paced with a frown on her face. "I don't know nobody way out there, Shemar. What will I do if I get out there and you kick me to the curb all the way? I'd be knocked down and drug all the way out. At least here I still have my father and my grandparents. Yeah, me and my father aren't on the best terms, but at least I know he'll be there if I need him to be." She tilted her face to the ceiling and exhaled real loudly.

I stood up and blocked her path, taking her hands within my own. "Listen to me, Simone. If I stay here, them people gonna lock me up for a long ass time, then they gon' kill me. Now, the only way for us to avoid all of this is if we leave and never come back down this way. You're the mother of my child, and I love you. You should be with me where I can make sure that you're well taken care of at all times. At least grant me that." I tried to pull her in to a hug, but she pushed me away. That hurt my heart.

"And what we gon' do out there, Shemar, huh? You gon' be with me. You gon' be my husband like you're supposed to be, now that we have a kid together? Or are you gon' keep on playin' these games that I can't afford to play?" She frowned and looked up at me. She curled her upper lip, then turned her back to me. "Sometimes, I can't stand you, and I hate how much I love yo' ass. I wish I never gave you my virginity because if I didn't, I don't think I would love you so hard." She shook her head.

I walked around and in front of her. "Simone, I am really trying here and I don't have it all the way figured out, but I know I'm supposed to hold you down and be there for you and my son as much as I can. I'm eighteen. You gotta give me just a little time to get my mind right so I can stand on my throne as a man for you. This version of man that you see right now ain't always gon' be this. Don't you understand that?" I asked, feeling some type of way.

I felt like she was looking at me like a buster or something. The way she kept on curling her lip made me feel like I disgusted her to her very core.

She looked up at me with those pretty brown eyes. The mole to left side of her cheek had always made her look so fine to me, and it still did. Every time I was in her presence I just wanted to do the right thing, but then as soon as Purity crossed my path, I just couldn't control myself. She was like a drug that had a hold on me. I didn't think I could ever let her go, nor did I want to. My love for her was beyond strong. It was a straight obsession.

"So, what are the odds of you leaving me once we get out there, Shemar? Then what are the odds of us getting married, once again, like we're supposed to be?" She blinked tears. "Seriously, I wanna know, because I feel like we're supposed to be married or God is going to keep punishing us."

I ran my hand over my face and tried to calm down. I couldn't think clearly enough without lying to her, and since I never had before, I wasn't about right then. "First of all, I'd never bring you all the way out there just to leave you. I'm not a trifling nigga like that. Far as the marriage go, I'm not really ready for that just yet, but when I am, it's going to be you. That I promise."

She wiped her tears from her cheeks and shook her head, sniffling. "You know what, Shemar? Even though I know you gon' hurt me out here, I'm gon' follow you because I love you and I know that deep down in my heart you're the man I'm supposed to be with for the rest of my life. You may not see it in me right now, but I am the wife for you, and I'll die trying to prove that to you." She stepped forward and laid her head on my chest. "Is Purity coming, too? I mean, I know she is, but I just want to hear you say it."

I rubbed her back. "Yeah, she coming. But don't worry, we'll all make this thing work."

I stood there, holding her for a long time, then I went out into the parking lot and told Nikki and

Purity to go and help her get packed, both the things in the hotel, and those back at our mother's house.

Purity shook her head. "This shit finna be crazy. Man, I hate she had your baby. Now we stuck with this bitch." She flung open her passenger's door and walked up to the hotel door and knocked on it, before crossing her arms across her chest and mugging me.

Nikki walked up to me and whispered, "Shemar, I hope you know what you doing?" She stood on her tippy toes and kissed my cheek.

Ghost

Chapter 15

The air was humid and so thick that I could barely breathe. I was sweating like a slave picking cotton in the middle of July as I sat down at the round table with Risky and five of his men that I had come to know over the last few months I'd been hustling with them. There were assault rifles on the table with clips so long they looked like Pez dispensers.

Risky cleared his throat with a mug on his face. "I ain't accepting what them bitch niggas did to my baby mama. I gotta make this shit right and I need you niggas to rollout to this fundraiser the Haitians having downtown on Cypress. Supposedly, they trying to lock down a few of the councilmen in our district. They taking this shit to a whole 'nother level that we ain't seen before, but I don't give a fuck about none of that. All that says to me is that they ain't gon' have no weapons with 'em. That fool Clef gon' be there, too. He the one the streets say put the hit on my baby mother that day we got caught slipping at the liquor store. If I don't kill no other nigga tonight, I gotta kill him, and I need you hittas to roll with me. You too, Shemar."

I looked around at these dumb ass niggas like they were crazy. "Are you serious? Y'all really trying to go shoot up some shit downtown when the city already on lockdown for some shit we done not even a week ago? How much sense do that make?" I questioned, looking Risky in the eyes.

This nigga had to be out of his mind. Whoever got away with shooting some shit downtown? I didn't give a fuck what city you were in, nine times out of ten, your downtown region of that city was the most secure. I already had the feds on my ass. Fucking around downtown was gon' get me killed before they could even snatch me up.

Risky slammed his hand on the table and stood with a grimaced look on his face. "So, what you saying, Shemar? You ain't rolling out with us? After all them times I had yo' back, the one time I need you to have mine, you ain't gon' answer the call for me?" He started to walk in my direction like he had something on his mind.

I knew the nigga didn't have it all, so I wasn't about to let him just run up on me like it was sweet. I jumped up and kicked my chair back. "Bruh, you heard what the fuck I said. Now I know you hurtin' over yo' baby mother gettin' hit up by these niggas but risking all our lives on this blank mission ain't gon' bring her back. This city is locked down because of us. If we go down to where all them white folks at, shooting and putting they life in danger, they gon' lynch our stupid asses, and they'd be well within their rights."

Risky upped his .45 and cocked it back with his nostrils flared. "Only thing I'm hearing right now is that you ain't rollin' with me and my niggas. So that means you the enemy just like them. And if that's the case, I might as well splash you right here and right now." He took a step back and pointed his pistol at my forehead. "I never really liked you, man. I always felt like Taurus put you on the throne too easily. How the fuck I been slaying niggas in Cloverland since I was twelve, then when it's time for me to move up the ranks after putting so much work in, Hood Rich and Taurus bump me out the way and give you the throne? Fuck that!" He spat on the side of me and lowered his eyes. "Fuck you got to say, nigga?"

I felt him press the barrel of the gun to my forehead a little harder, and that shit made me mad. I always felt that he looked at me a little weird, especially whenever his baby mother was around me, but I never thought that in the back of his mind he was feeling like I stole his throne.

I leaned my head back and swallowed. "So, just because I'm telling you that what you thinking about doing ain't smart, you wanna waste me? Nigga, ever since I met you I been one hundred with you. I ain't got shit against you or yo' niggas. I thought we was all family. One love."

Honestly, I didn't give a fuck about na'n one of them niggas in that room. I was saying what I had to because this fuck nigga had me at gunpoint, and all his niggas were armed with assault rifles. I was in a no-win situation and I couldn't take that L like that. I had to be smart and outthink this idiot ass nigga because, at the end of the day, I was all that my family of women had to depend on. Them and my son.

Risky laughed. "Yeah, nigga, it's funny how this heat will humble a nigga. You walking around Cloverland like you run that muhfucka, not knowing that if it wasn't for me, killas would have been knocked yo' head off. You ain't Cloverland, nigga! I am! I been running my muthafuckin' city! Way before Hood Rich, way before Taurus! Them niggas ain't even from Houston. Taurus from Memphis and Hood Rich dead ass is from Chicago! That ain't even the south, my nigga." He grabbed me by the throat and slammed me against the wall aggressively, putting his face close to mine. Close enough for me to smell his stanking ass breath. "You know what, Shemar, I'm taking over this throne and my city. Where them birds at, nigga? Where is yo' stash. I gotta have all dat and it might just keep me from whacking yo' pretty boy ass." He guffawed at his own remark, and his hittas joined in.

My nose flared. I was starting to lose my cool. Once I lost my temper, I knew I was gon' make these niggas kill me. I could only take so much of being treated like a bitch. I was a goon by DNA. This fuck shit wasn't in me.

I snickered. "You always calling me a pretty boy. That mean I'm soft, right?" I laughed at his punk ass.

"That's exactly what it means. Like I said before, had I not kept them killas off yo' ass, you'd be a dead nigga already. Now tell me where them birds at. I ain't gon' ask you again." He jacked me up a little more.

"Nigga, I'll tell you what. Since I'm so soft, how 'bout you put that pistol down and fight me, fist for fist. I bet I'd whoop yo' ass in front of yo' niggas. But if you whoop me, I'll take you to all three of my stash spots and empty them bitches, then turn over the throne to you as a man. What you think about that?" I asked, feeling his knuckles dig into my neck.

He squinted. "Aw, you think it's sweet. Nigga, you ain't said nothing but a word." He turned around and tossed the pistol to his right-hand man. "Bruh, I'm finna beat the shit out of this nigga, and then we finna empty his safes. I need to take my aggression out on a muhfucka's ass anyway." He took a step back, bent down and tied his shoes. He jumped up and got to bouncing on his toes with his guards up. "Y'all don't jump in either. Let me whoop this nigga on my own." He walked toward me slowly, covering his chin.

I watched his niggas scoot the table back and push it against the wall. Then they stepped away, giving us room to fight.

"Let's go, bitch nigga! Throw yo' guards up." He took a step forward to swing on me, and as soon as he did, I upped my .38 Special, cocked the hammer and let that bitch ride all in his face.

Boom! Boom! Boom!

The bullets knocked half of his head off right away, spraying his brains against the wall. His hittas looked so shocked that for a moment they froze, looking stupid as hell, and that's when I unloaded on them. *Boom! Boom! Boom!* Finally, I took off running up the stairs and out of the building with them on my ass.

When I get outside, the sun was on full blast. There was a crowd of people standing outside of the building, and kids all in the street throwing a football back and forth to one another. The crowd disbursed when they saw me run out of the building like a mad man.

"That bitch ass nigga just killed Risky. Get his ass, man!" Somebody hollered behind me before the shots went off.

Thot-thot-thot-thot! Boom! Boom! Boom! Boom! Thot-thot-thot! I could feel the bullets flying past me as I ran in the direction of my car. I felt my heart getting ready to leap out of my chest. I kept on running, ducked as low to the ground as I could possibly get while maintaining my balance.

Boom! Boom! Boom! Boom! Tsssssh! The back window to my whip shattered, just as I got to the driver's door. The kids that were in the middle of the street scattered while a bunch of people screamed off in the distance. I looked over my shoulder to see about three dudes running full speed in my direction with guns in their hands. I popped the locks with my keychain and flung open the door, diving in, just as they got about twenty yards away from it, and really let loose. *Boom! Boom! Boom! Boom!*

I felt the car rocking as the windows shattered all around me, falling on my back, and into my shirt. I waited for the shots to stop, then threw the key in the ignition and stormed away from the curb, smacking a nigga with a kay that was running across the street in my direction. I could hear him scream out as the car rolled over him. Behind me, the shots continued to come until I turned the corner and wound up on the busy street a block away.

From there, I jumped on the highway just as my phone buzzed with a text from Taurus. It read, *"What's good? Why you been blowin' me up?"* I stepped on the gas and tried my best to text him with one hand, telling him to pick up the phone.

As soon as he did, I tried to tell him everything at once. After I finished, he told me to meet him at his mansion at three in the morning; he would be back in town then, and it was important that we met face to face. That sent a chill down my spine because I didn't know what the homie had on his mind. I was hoping that he wasn't thinking I was deadweight or something, so I told him I would be there. Before I even hung up the phone, a text came through from Nikki, telling me to rush to my mother's house right away.

When I got there, Nikki opened the door and I ran inside, hoping for the best.

Nikki slammed the door and locked it, grabbed my hand and pulled me toward the back of the house. "Shemar, you ain't finna believe this shit. Please know that I couldn't prevent it if I tried to. When I came in the house, they were already fighting, and I couldn't get in between them, or I would have gotten fucked up myself. I don't want you to be mad at me, and just know that I'm with you one hundred percent with whatever you wanna do. Just please don't be mad at me." Nikki cried as she stopped in front of my mother's old room and stepped out of the way.

I scrunched my face, looking her up and down like she had lost her mind. When I pushed open the door, I nearly passed out. Purity was sitting on the edge of my mother's bed with her head down.

In her hands was a steak knife dripping with blood. On the floor, directly beneath her feet, was Simone. Her shirt was bloody. Her eyes closed, and she kept on jerking on the carpet with traces of blood drooling out of the corner of her mouth. I saw that she had at least ten big holes in her shirt.

When Purity heard the door open she jumped off the bed and put her hands in the air. "Look, Shemar, she came at me with this knife. If I hadn't taken it and used it against her, I would have been where she is right now," she said with tears rolling down her cheeks. She got up to wrap her arms around me.

I dropped to my knees and picked Simone's head up onto my lap. I ran my hand over her stab wounds and tried to stop them from bleeding. "Simone. Baby, please don't die. I'm so sorry!" I hollered looking into her struggling face.

She tried to talk, but only coughed up a mouth full of blood. Her eyes rolled into the back of her head. She started to shake uncontrollably.

"Shemar, I need you. I'm sorry. I didn't mean too. Please hug me or I'm about to die." Purity whimpered and dropped to her knees beside me. I felt her trying to lay her head on my shoulder, and I jerked away from her.

In that moment, I didn't want to be touched. I still loved her, and I knew I would wind up consoling her later, but in that moment, I couldn't focus in on her emotions. In my arms, my son's mother was dying. A woman that had been nothing but good to me from the first day that I was accepted into her home by her mother and father. I had failed this woman miserably, and I felt lower than scum.

My son started to scream and holler somewhere in the house. Nikki disappeared and came back with him, bouncing him up and down on her hip until he calmed down.

I laid my cheek onto Simone's, feeling my heart break in half. "Simone, please fight through this, baby. Please don't die. I'll do anything you want. Just please, stay here with me." I cried with tears running down my face and dripping from my chin.

Purity crawled closer to me and tried once again to put her head on my shoulder. "Shemar, please talk to me. Tell me that you love me, Shemar, because I need to hear it. Please, I need you. Bad." She wrapped her arm around my neck and kissed me on the cheek. I could feel her wet tears drip on to my arm.

I sat up and looked into Simone's face. Her eyes were wide open and unseeing. Her chest no longer rose and fell. There were no more words that she tried to force out unsuccessfully. She was now as still as a board, and it was then that I felt like a dagger had been stabbed into my heart.

I closed her eyes and kissed her on the forehead before laying my cheek back against hers. I needed to soak in her warmth. I felt so sick. I didn't know what to do.

Nikki stepped into front of us and leaned down with the baby in her hands. "Shemar, that girl dead. I know you're hurting, but we gotta get the fuck out of here right now or we're all going to prison. Let's be smart, baby, please," she begged, bouncing Junior up and down.

Purity tried to wrap her arms all the way around me. "Shemar, I need you, big bruh. I need you. I'm hurting right now. Can you please hug me? Please, show me some love or I don't know what I'll do to myself." She broke into a fit of tears and coughing spells.

I hugged Simone tighter and cried into her bloody chest. "Purity, not right now! Can't you see that I just lost my son's mother? She's dead! What the fuck am

I going to do now? Huh?" I hollered, pushing her slightly away from me.

That was the wrong move. "No! Please! Don't push me away. You're my everything. I need you so bad. Please, Shemar, just hug me." She cried with snot running out of her nose. She grabbed my arm and I pushed her away from me. She fell to her stomach and cried into the carpet, before getting up and leaving the room. "I can't take it anymore!" She screamed.

I didn't care. Emotionally, I wasn't there. I didn't know what she was going to attempt to do to herself, but in that moment, I just really didn't care.

I felt Simone's blood saturating my clothes and it was all I could think about. I had failed our mother. Failed her as a protector. My sins had finally caught up with me and I felt worse than I ever had before. I didn't know how I was going to carry on in life with the guilt of her death. I felt like I didn't even deserve to keep on breathing, but then I looked up at my son and I felt my heart skip a beat.

He was the last surviving portion of Simone and my mother. I needed to be around for him. To protect him and give him the love that I should have been rendered unconditionally unto his mother.

Nikki must've known what I was thinking, because as I held Simone's corpse in my arms, she kneeled and brought Junior closer to me so his cheek could rub against mine while the other laid against his mother's.

"We'll get through this, Shemar. I'll be there for you however you need me to be. But we have to get up out of here," Nikki said, then wrapped her arm around my neck. With her doing that, we were all somehow physically connected with my cheek against Simone's and my son's, then her arm around me, and her face in the crux of my neck.

I closed my eyes and let the tears flow out of me.

We must've stayed that way in silence for what must've been five minutes when the door to the bedroom was kicked open. The loud bang made me open my eyes and look up and into the distraught face of Purity.

She held Nikki's .45 that she kept under her driver's seat, in her hands. "I knew you loved her more than me, Shemar. Nobody loves me anymore. You were all I had! All I ever needed!" She screamed.

Nikki started to get up but couldn't quite make it to her feet before the shots started coming in our direction. *Boom! Boom! Boom! Boom!*

"Ahhhhhh!" Nikki had caught four bullets to her chest, dropping her to the floor.

"Purity!"

"No, Shemar! Fuck that! I'm tired of mafuckas not loving me."

"But, Purity—"

Boom!

"Ahhh, shit! What the fuck!" She lodged a bullet into my lower abdomen. I held my son tighter, trying my best to shield him.

"I'm so sorry, Shemar. I'm so sorry. I just wanted you to love me. *Only me*."

"I do, Purity. I promise, I do. Don't do this." Man, a nigga couldn't go out like this.

"No! You. Don't." *Boom! Boom!* She fired two shots to my upper body, sending me to the ground with me still struggling to keep my son safe.

My vision became blurry and the ringing in my ears seemed to grow louder.

"I'm so sorry, Shemar." I heard her say through sobs. "I hope you can forgive me. I forgive you."

Boom!

All I remember was hearing my son's screams in the background, and witnessing the sickening sight of Purity's lifeless body. Then, everything faded to black.

Now I see how some lines should never be crossed. It ain't a game when it comes to matters of the heart. Just look where it got me.

The End.

Submission Guideline.

Submit the first three chapters of your completed manuscript to ldpsubmissions@gmail.com, subject line: Your book's title. The manuscript must be in a .doc file and sent as an attachment. Document should be in Times New Roman, double spaced and in size 12 font. Also, provide your synopsis and full contact information. If sending multiple submissions, they must each be in a separate email.

Have a story but no way to send it electronically? You can still submit to LDP/Ca$h Presents. Send in the first three chapters, written or typed, of your completed manuscript to:

LDP: Submissions Dept
Po Box 870494
Mesquite, Tx 75187

DO NOT send original manuscript. Must be a duplicate.

Provide your synopsis and a cover letter containing your full contact information.

Thanks for considering LDP and Ca$h Presents.

<u>Coming Soon from Lock Down Publications/Ca$h Presents</u>

BOW DOWN TO MY GANGSTA

By **Ca$h**

TORN BETWEEN TWO

By **Coffee**

BLOOD STAINS OF A SHOTTA **III**

By **Jamaica**

WHEN THE STREETS CLAP BACK **III**

By **Jibril Williams**

STEADY MOBBIN

By **Marcellus Allen**

BLOOD OF A BOSS **V**

By **Askari**

WHEN A GOOD GIRL GOES BAD **II**

By **Adrienne**

THE HEART OF A GANGSTA **III**

By **Jerry Jackson**

LOYAL TO THE GAME **IV**

By **T.J. & Jelissa**

A DOPEBOY'S PRAYER **II**

By **Eddie "Wolf" Lee**

IF LOVING YOU IS WRONG… **III**

LOVE ME EVEN WHEN IT HURTS

By **Jelissa**

DAUGHTERS OF A SAVAGE

By **Chris Green**

BLOODY COMMAS **III**

SKI MASK CARTEL II

By **T.J. Edwards**

TRAPHOUSE KING

By **Hood Rich**

BLAST FOR ME **II**

RAISED AS A GOON V

By **Ghost**

A DISTINGUISHED THUG STOLE MY HEART **III**

By **Meesha**

ADDICTIED TO THE DRAMA **II**

By **Jamila Mathis**

LIPSTICK KILLAH II

By **Mimi**

THE BOSSMAN'S DAUGHTERS 4

WHAT BAD BITCHES DO

By **Aryanna**

Available Now

RESTRAINING ORDER **I & II**

By **CA$H & Coffee**

LOVE KNOWS NO BOUNDARIES **I II & III**

By **Coffee**

RAISED AS A GOON I, II, III & IV

BRED BY THE SLUMS I, II

BLAST FOR ME

By **Ghost**

LAY IT DOWN **I & II**

LAST OF A DYING BREED

BLOOD STAINS OF A SHOTTA I & II

By **Jamaica**

LOYAL TO THE GAME

LOYAL TO THE GAME II

LOYAL TO THE GAME III

By **TJ & Jelissa**

BLOODY COMMAS I & II

SKI MASK CARTEL

By **T.J. Edwards**

IF LOVING HIM IS WRONG…I & II

By **Jelissa**

WHEN THE STREETS CLAP BACK

By **Jibril Williams**

A DISTINGUISHED THUG STOLE MY HEART I & II

By **Meesha**

PUSH IT TO THE LIMIT

By **Bre' Hayes**

BLOOD OF A BOSS **I, II, III & IV**

By **Askari**

THE STREETS BLEED MURDER **I, II & III**

THE HEART OF A GANGSTA I & II

By **Jerry Jackson**

CUM FOR ME

CUM FOR ME 2

CUM FOR ME 3

An **LDP Erotica Collaboration**

BRIDE OF A HUSTLA **I & II**

THE FETTI GIRLS **I, II& III**

By **Destiny Skai**

WHEN A GOOD GIRL GOES BAD

By **Adrienne**

A GANGSTER'S REVENGE **I II III & IV**

THE BOSS MAN'S DAUGHTERS

THE BOSS MAN'S DAUGHTERS II

THE BOSSMAN'S DAUGHTERS III

A SAVAGE LOVE **I & II**

BAE BELONGS TO ME

A HUSTLER'S DECEIT I, II

By **Aryanna**

A KINGPIN'S AMBITON

A KINGPIN'S AMBITION **II**

I MURDER FOR THE DOUGH

By **Ambitious**

TRUE SAVAGE

TRUE SAVAGE II

TRUE SAVAGE **III**

By **Chris Green**

A DOPEBOY'S PRAYER

By **Eddie "Wolf" Lee**

THE KING CARTEL **I, II & III**

By **Frank Gresham**

THESE NIGGAS AIN'T LOYAL **I, II & III**

By **Nikki Tee**

GANGSTA SHYT **I II &III**

By **CATO**

THE ULTIMATE BETRAYAL

By **Phoenix**

BOSS'N UP **I , II & III**

By **Royal Nicole**

I LOVE YOU TO DEATH

By Destiny J

I RIDE FOR MY HITTA

I STILL RIDE FOR MY HITTA

By **Misty Holt**

LOVE & CHASIN' PAPER

By **Qay Crockett**

TO DIE IN VAIN

By **ASAD**

BROOKLYN HUSTLAZ

By **Boogsy Morina**

BROOKLYN ON LOCK I & II

By **Sonovia**

GANGSTA CITY

By **Teddy Duke**

A DRUG KING AND HIS DIAMOND

A DOPEMAN'S RICHES

By Nicole Goosby

BOOKS BY LDP'S CEO, CA$H

TRUST IN NO MAN

TRUST IN NO MAN 2

TRUST IN NO MAN 3

BONDED BY BLOOD

SHORTY GOT A THUG

THUGS CRY

THUGS CRY 2

THUGS CRY 3

TRUST NO BITCH

TRUST NO BITCH 2

TRUST NO BITCH 3

TIL MY CASKET DROPS

RESTRAINING ORDER

RESTRAINING ORDER 2

IN LOVE WITH A CONVICT

Coming Soon

BONDED BY BLOOD 2

BOW DOWN TO MY GANGSTA

Ghost

200

Printed in the USA
CPSIA information can be obtained
at www.ICGtesting.com
CBHW071210210124
3648CB00008B/472